THE UNRAVELLING

THE UNRAVELING

A Collection of Short Horror Stories

The Unraveling

A Collection of Short Horror Stories

Copyright © 2020 The Writers' Cache

Print ISBN: 978-1-7360125-0-5

Cover images copyright Tithi Luadthong

Cover design copyright The Writers' Cache

 Created with Vellum

Contents

Slender

Chadd VanZanten

THE GUY at the lumber store intimidates me. He's about my age, but he's one of these rugged types. Big shoulders, good jawline. He jumps off his forklift and comes over.

I say, "Hi. How's it going?" I'm getting ready to tell him a lie. A lot of lies.

He says, "What can I help you with?"

That's all it takes to put me on the defensive. The clipped, curt reply. His namebadge says *Chris*, and he's here to help me. Because I can't help myself. I'm helpless.

Chris pulls off his leather work gloves, jams them in the back pocket of his Levis. They dangle out in a really rugged way, but I've been practicing my technique, so I'm okay for now.

I learned about lying from a movie about this guy who has to lie to the FBI to save his daughter. See, the guy knows who kidnapped her, and the FBI are going to ask him, but if he tells the FBI, the kidnapper will kill her before they catch him. So, the guy stands in front of a full-length mirror for hours and hours, practicing the lie.

I hand Chris the key and say it just like I practiced: "I just need a copy of this."

He tells me to follow him. You see what I mean, right? He's in charge. I follow him. As he escorts me from the lumber yard to the key copying machine, he taps the key with the back of his rugged middle finger, and says, "This has *DO NOT DUPLICATE* stamped on it."

In this other movie I saw, there was a woman who cheats on her husband, and her sister helps her cover it up. The sister says if you're going to tell one lie, might as well tell lots of lies. See, most people think it's dangerous to lie because you have to tell another lie to cover it up, and another to cover that one. The sister says the more lies there are, the harder it will be for them to find the lie you actually want to tell.

So I say, "Oh, I forgot about that." Lie Number One. "I put that on all my keys." Number two. "I guess I could go find a spare that's not stamped, but you'd be closed by the time I got back, and I was hoping to have this for my girlfriend tonight. She's moving in. We just got engaged." Three, four, five, six.

Chris eyes me. I've never really had a girlfriend, and if Chris would look a little more carefully, he'd figure that out. I basically stopped putting on weight at age fifteen. I'm very, very slender, and not in the good way. I'm a little taller than Chris, but if I stood behind him, you wouldn't see any part of me except the top of my head.

He says, "You put that on here?"

I realize now that was a hole in my cover story. How do you get *DO NOT DUPLICATE* on a key? Do you have to have a locksmith do it? Or can you do it yourself? Either way, it's a great policy. It was pretty easy for me to steal the key, but putting *DO NOT DUPLICATE* on all the spare keys is a massively decent back-up plan. So, whoever did that—good job. It's not your fault it didn't work.

Sure, I could say, "Yeah, I stamped it on there—with my *DO NOT DUPLICATE* stamp." But I know saying "yes" when the answer is "no" is the easiest lie to spot. Learned it in a movie about this military interrogator who's trying to get one critical piece of information from a terrorist, but the terrorist refuses to tell any real, direct lies. See, a really good liar doesn't just lie and lie and lie, he stays with the truth as long as he can.

So, I say, "No, a locksmith put that on there. You know, in case the keys get swiped. This town's full of criminals. For all I know, you're one of them."

Chris gives me a fake chuckle and says, "Right." Then he holds the key right up to his nose and squints at it. "It's just that this looks like some kind of master."

There are some things movies just can't teach you. Like how to think fast.

I straighten my collar and say, "That's what my lady tells me every night."

Chris laughs, for real this time. He grins his rugged grin. Usually, I wouldn't be able to get a laugh out of a guy like him, but I swear he was this close to fist-bumping me. I got lucky on that one, and if there's one thing movies have taught me, it's that luck counts for a lot.

Like finding the little gray metal box bolted to the wall down in the boiler room of my building. Pure luck. I mean, what are the chances? I guess the manager hid it down there, and it had to be long before I showed up because it's got an inch of dust on top. I've seen the huge ring of keys he keeps with him, but I never knew he had spares for all of them there in the boiler room. A hundred keys on hooks with labels. *UTITLY.*

STORAGE. ROOF. MASTER. The box has a lock on it, too, but it was unlocked. Really, what are the chances of that?

Funny thing is there's a spare key in the box labeled *KEY BOX*, which means if the manager ever lost the original, he'd either have an extra key for a box he never locks, or an extra key inside a box he can't unlock.

Chris takes another close-up look at the key. I shouldn't have given it to him right away. I should have asked him if he would copy it first. This is why I came to the lumber yard instead of a locksmith—I was hoping they wouldn't know or care about the rules. I'm vague on the legalities here. Can he ask me for ID? Can he keep the key and report me somehow?

But then he asks, "You're sure this is your key, right?"

"Yeah, I'm pretty sure it's mine," I say, laughing my very best relaxed chuckle, but Chris is already picking out the key blank for me. Probably needs to get back to his forklift.

He screws the original into one vise and the blank goes in the other. The motor spins up. It's too loud to talk, so we stand there trying to find something to look at while the screeching blade of the machine cuts into the brass duplicate. Chris unscrews the original and hands it to me, and I close my fist tight around it as the motor winds down. I shove the original into my pocket, way down to the bottom. Then Chris drops the copied key into my hand.

"Careful," he says. "It's still hot."

I thought it was just my imagination, but it is hot. It burns me a little. I bounce it on my palm.

"Let's go up to the register," says Chris. "Get you checked out."

I follow him, past the plywood and insulation, past the paint. He doesn't say anything or even act like he knows I'm behind him.

As we get to the cash registers I say, "Can I ask you a quick question?"

"Yeah."

"You put *DO NOT DUPLICATE* on a key so that if it gets stolen, someone can't make a copy and then return the original, right?"

Chris shrugs. "Right."

"Well, that's a good policy and all, but, how do you know that's not what I did?"

He laughs.

I laugh, too. Then I say, "Seriously, though."

"Well. I guess I don't." Now he's on the defensive. He gets behind a cash register. I can tell he's nervous. Chris is nervous. Forklift Chris. The guy who can be rugged just by shoving workgloves into his back pocket. He says: "But, I mean, what's the worst that could happen?"

Last night I watched this movie about a mafia guy who goes against his bosses and then has to lie about it. This was the best one. The guy knows if his bosses catch him, they'll kill him, and he knows the bosses are good at spotting liars because they do it a couple times earlier in the movie. So, he tells the cops he'll give them information about the mafia if they help him lie to his bosses.

Here's what the cops teach him: when you say the lie, think the truth. And they put a polygraph on him to test him.

See, most people try to push the truth out of their head when they lie, but that's wrong. If you're going to lie, you have to fill yourself with the truth.

"The worst?" I pause, but only for effect. "The worst is that I stole the master key and a bunch of people in my apartment building are going to end up raped, murdered, chopped up, and buried in the basement. That's the worst."

Chris laughs again, but he's looking up at me and he's not rugged at all anymore.

I look at him straight in the face. He fiddles with the cash register.

"Okay, okay," he says, "but what are the chances of that?"

"Slender," I tell him. "Very, very slender."

2

Three Dead Things: A Found Story

Alexander Gordon Smith

Taken from *This Book Will Kill You*

IT WAS my brother Frank who took me to see the three dead things.

"I found them last night," Frank told me as we walked through the woods behind our farm. "Daniel told me they was there and he was right."

Daniel, Frank's friend from school. The same guy who told Frank that aliens built the Pyramids and that dogs can read your thoughts. Nothing Daniel said was ever true, but Frank believed all of it, every word of it. He's twelve, too, two years older than me, old enough to know better.

"Daniel says you can't go looking for them," said Frank. "Daniel says you only find them when you're lost. But I remember."

He taps his head, his grin as bright as the sun through the tops of the trees.

"I made a map, in my head."

But as usual, Frank's head didn't work right. We walked for an hour before he admitted he didn't know where we were, and that the three dead things weren't where he thought they'd been the day before. And almost as soon as he admitted it I saw one of them staring at me. I got a mighty jolt of my heart, for sure, because I could have sworn I saw it move, like it was rolling into position behind a yew tree, peeking at me through the leaves. But when we got closer, Frank grinning even harder now, I saw that it couldn't have moved because it was made of wood, rooted in place by decades of undergrowth.

It was a statue, twice as tall as me and shaped like a bird. Frank told me that Daniel told him it was a skylark, but I wouldn't know. It was standing upright, its eyes staring into the forest, its beak covered up by its wings, which were folded over the bottom of its face. It must have been standing there for close to forever because its wooden body was warped and green with lichen, but when Frank pointed to the bottom of the statue I could still see the door there in the weeds, two-foot square with a little wooden latch.

"They've all come," Frank said, nodding at something over my shoulder. I think I've stood on an ant's nest because my skin itches all over. When I turn I see two other statues crowding around us, facing inward, as old as the first and rooted to the ground like trees. They're so close I don't know how I didn't see them to start with, and I'm not lying when I say there's something kicking in my gut, something telling me that this part of the forest is too old, too dead, for me to be here.

The second statue is a rabbit, maybe a hare because the ears are longer, its paws stuffed into them. Its eyes seem somehow full of grief, whoever made this thing has hacked lines into them, into its brow. Its mouth is open but they look more like horse's teeth than rabbit ones. It too has a little door at the base of it, shut tight.

I'm not sure what the final statue is supposed to be. It has the body of a sheep, maybe, sitting upright on its haunches. But its hands are human, and enormous, big enough to curl over the whole top half of its head like it's trying to pull off its own scalp. I can't see its eyes, and its mouth is just a line half-visible beneath its thin wrists. Two short, stubby horns jut out over its ears. This, too, had a door, and this door was open—just a crack, mind.

I wanted to leave. There are some places that you know almost instantly are wrong. They're places where bad things have happened, places that want bad things to happen. I felt those statues watching us and it wasn't an illusion. They knew we were there. They were so old, so still, and they knew we were there.

I asked Frank if we could leave but he shook his head. He had that look on his face, the one where he was going to hurt me. Not physically; he would never have done that, but he wanted to play a trick. That's what big brothers do, I know, and Frank's tricks were almost always harmless. But it wasn't like I'd be able to find my way back by myself and the night was stirring, the sun falling fast.

"Daniel says there are two dead girls beneath the ground here," Frank said, relishing it. "They've been here a long, long time, and they are so lonely."

I begged him to stop, I was even crying now, but tears are like a red rag to brothers.

"They were murdered by their mother," he went on. "She harvested them, and left the rest here for the crows. Their father, driven mad by grief, built three statues to remember them. The first for his oldest daughter, who he called his little Leveret." He pointed to the hare. "She died last, Daniel says, and she had to watch her sister pass first. The younger daughter was as thin and carefree as a bird, so he gave her this statue."

I thought I heard the wood crack, like a swaying tree, and I pleaded with Frank, trying to pull him back to the path. But he was so much bigger than me, so much stronger.

"Daniel says the father hunted down his wife and killed her, to avenge his daughters. He brought her here and buried her beneath the third statue, so that she would forever have to live with the horror of what she did."

Another crack of wood, and I thought that maybe one of the fingers of the third statue had moved, because wasn't that the corner of an eye I saw now between them? I backed away, ready to escape by myself, but Daniel grabbed my arm and held me.

"Don't you want to know about the doors?" he said, his eyes full of glee. I nod, even though I don't want to know about the doors. I don't even want to look at the doors. "Daniel says the father left the doors there because he knew that he would always have a way to speak with his children. And he left a door in his wife's so that she would never be able to rest."

I noticed how quiet the woods were; no birds singing, no wind in the branches, just another of those bone-shaking cracks. I swore I could see more of the third statue's eye now through its fingers, dark and wet.

"Daniel says that if you're brave enough to go inside, you'll see the dead," Frank said, and as soon as he said this the reality of what was about to happen exploded in my skull, so bright I couldn't see. "And they'll tell you a secret."

"No," was all I could say, but Frank was hauling me to the first statue, the bird.

"Inside the skylark you will meet the first daughter," he said. "And she will ask you a question, but you must not reply."

I was hysterical now. I was hitting him with my fists.

"Inside the hare, you will hear the second daughter whisper to you, but you must not listen."

We were so close, and the statues seemed closer still, like they were herding us in.

"And inside that one, the bad one, the mother will lie down beside you but you must not look at her. If you do all these things then you will learn something incredible."

I lashed out again and my fist connected with his lip. He let go, swearing and I fell, scuttling backwards. I was scared, because I'd never hurt Frank before, I didn't know what he would do to punish me. He was mad, spitting blood from the wound I had opened up on his mouth, but he did not move to hit me back.

"Fine," he said. "Coward. You stay right there and watch, and when they tell me their secret I won't let you know, I won't. Daniel says he did it and the secret blew his mind. I'm going to know it too and you won't."

I called his name, I asked him to come home with me, to leave the statues alone, but he had a look in his eye I'd never really seen before. His head had always been a little bit broken but this was something new. He didn't even look like my brother any more as he gently lifted the latch and the first door opened. I don't think I've ever seen darkness like that. It was an impossible kind of darkness, it seemed to bleed out of that door and embrace him.

He was almost too big to get inside, but somehow he managed it. I hate myself, because I just watched it happen. I just let him shuffle his body through the dirt until all that was left was the soles of his trainers. Then they too vanished into the shadows.

I don't know how long I waited. It might have been minutes, maybe even an hour. By the time I gathered the strength to move it was almost dark, and Frank was still inside the statue. He did not respond to my calls, and when I plunged my arm inside the door I could not feel him at all, even though there was barely enough room for him to lie down inside it.

I can't describe the fear I felt right then. Part of me knew that Frank was joking, that he was waiting in there for me to start screaming, and then he would burst out and howl at me the way he always did.

But part of me knew, too, that I was never going to see my brother again. Part of me knew that the girl inside had asked him a question and the idiot had answered her, that he'd sunk down into the leaves, into the moss, into a little nest of twigs and bones.

I still did it. I still got down on my knees next to that little door and began to crawl inside. He was my brother, you see, and I loved him, I loved him enough to crawl into this dead thing and call his name. It was like a coffin, no space to do anything other than push my face and chest to the dirt and wiggle forward. I could smell forest mulch, dirt, rotting wood, and the damp crept into my clothes, into my bones. It was hard to breathe, but I still worked up enough courage to call Frank's name, reaching out for him. None of the day came in with me, and I could not even turn my head to see if the door was still open. I just inched my way forward, surely too far, surely far enough to have emerged from the back of the statue. Except it kept going, and going, the space growing smaller and smaller and smaller.

I had to stop or lose my mind, and it was only when I lay

there, gasping, no air for me to breathe, that I heard a voice. It came from right beside me, and I became aware of a shape in the dark, soft and cold. It pressed into me and I would have screamed if I could remember how. A pair of lips brushed against my ear and I heard the same whisper once again.

Do you want to know where he went?

My mouth was open to answer but I remembered Frank's words. I clamped my lips shut while that corpse-cold body folded itself around me, while stiff fingers felt my face, while it breathed its grave-stench into me.

Do you want to know where he went?

It asked the same question a dozen times but each time I stayed still, stayed quiet, until I felt the shape of her roll away. I escaped that statue with such violence that I was bleeding in three or four places. I slammed the door shut and clicked the latch into place, running from the clearing. I only looked back once to see all three statues facing me, all of them watching me go—two through wide, sad eyes, the third through the open fingers of its hands.

I know you will hate me for what I did. I hate myself, god only knows it. I wish I had had the courage to search for him in the other two statues, because maybe that's the secret I would have learned. My mother and father hate me, too, because even though I've never spoken a word of what happened to anybody, they sense it. They see the giant holes in between my words, they feel the abyss of unspeakable truth there, in the space between the lies. They know that Frank did not run away, that he did not fall into an old mine, that he wasn't bundled into a white panel van. They know something far worse happened to him, and they know I will never tell them what it was. They know that they will die not knowing what happened to their son.

I cannot, because I do not know what it was. I will never know. And maybe you will forgive me a little if I told you I did go back. I searched for those statues for weeks, armed with a torch, and with Frank's instructions. But I never found them. I never found him.

And I will pay for my crime for the rest of my life. Because even though I never found Frank, he found me. He finds me every night, when I close my eyes. I wake inside the mouldering coffin of my bedsheets, his cold body pressed against mine, his lips breathing the same hoarse words right into my ear, over and over and over until dawn breaks.

Do you know where I am?

Do you know where I am?

Do you know where I am?

I never answer. I never answer him.

Alexander Gordon Smith, "Three Dead Things," first appeared in *This Book Will Kill You*, 2019. Reprinted with permission.

3

One For Sorrow

E.B. Wheeler

I HATE MISSING-PERSON CASES. Granted, I don't enjoy busting meth labs or breaking up domestic disputes, but at least there's closure: a sense that the world is a little safer now. But missing persons cases hang there, files never closed, defying neatness and order. Haunting me.

Take the one on my desk right now. Dr. Jenny Blake. African-American, medium-dark skin, long braids. Age 34. Just stopping over on her way back from L.A. for a pediatricians' conference. She checked in to the hotel at six and walked to the neighboring Denny's for dinner. Nothing odd about her behavior there. I've already interviewed the hostess and wait-ress. Then she walked back to the hotel. That's where things get weird.

I've got the footage from the security cameras. Her pace is casual as she approaches the lobby door, and she slows to dig in her purse. For gum? Her room key? She stops. Looks out over the desert. The sunset highlights dark streetlamps and the birds resting on the power lines. There's not much to see out there: just sagebrush, the outline of worn black rocks from long-extinct volcanoes, maybe a jackrabbit.

Jenny sort of nods, like she's listening to something. I've checked all the angles, including the stores across the street. She was alone. No one out there in the dusk. She glances up and makes eye contact with the security camera. Her eyes meet mine for a moment. Like she's making a decision. Or saying goodbye. Then she walks off into the desert. Just like that. The cameras from the back of the hotel catch one last glimpse of her, wandering off into the darkness. A blur in the night. Vanishing.

We pinged her cellphone, hoping to narrow down her location. Searchers found her purse not far from the hotel, sitting on the twisted trunk of a dead Joshua tree. Just set there like she meant to come back for it. No sign of a struggle. The phone still had a charge. But there was no other trace of Jenny Blake. We're still combing the desert, but it's vast and unforgiving, and it's been a week.

It's not illegal to walk away from your life. Jenny or any of the rest of us has the right to drop our briefcases or purses and just go. But she left behind a husband and two kids. Her practice was thriving, and everything indicates she loved her work. She wasn't on any medications, had no history of mental illness. No known enemies or financial problems. We still have to assume she's in danger, if not from herself or someone else, at least from the desert.

And now, I have to meet with the family again. Her husband has gone back to his hotel with the kids for the night, but her mother and sister have come back to the station, hoping for an update.

"Hi, John." Officer Hernandez smiles at me from her desk—

a sympathetic smile. The only bright spot in this day. I wrap it up to mull over later. I'm going to need it.

I step into a little waiting room with a couple of old brown couches and a coffee machine. The two women glance up, fear and desperate hope lining their faces.

"Have you found anything?" Jenny's mother asks quietly.

I sit across from them. "I'm sorry, but there's nothing new."

Jenny's sister breaks. Curls up in her seat with sobs shaking her body. Her mother lowers her head, defeated.

"We'll keep searching." My words sound empty, even to me.

Jenny's mom meets my eyes. "Why? Why would she leave?"

I shake my head. This is the worst part of missing-person cases. The unanswered questions. The realization that, beneath the facade of daily activities, of text messages and Facebook posts and family dinners, maybe we don't really know anybody. Secrets hide behind every face, buried so deep some of us might not know our own darkest corners, except in fragments of strange dreams. Sometimes it's other people's secrets that hurt us, but usually it's our own.

It's dark by the time I leave the station. A bird croaks, and I jump. A magpie perches in the tree outside the station, watching over the parking lot, probably drawn by the flood-lights. The white of its wings stands out in the shadows, but the night swallows the bird's black body. What is that saying about magpies? One for sorrow, two for joy?

We've had enough sorrow.

"Beat it!" I call, and the bird flies off, its wings a bright flash in the darkness.

———

The magpie is waiting when I show up in the morning. He's not alone this time. Three of the damn things sit in their tree, watching me. I try to wave them away with my Starbucks cup, but they're not intimidated.

Three. Three magpies. One is for sorrow, two is for joy. There's more to the nursery rhyme than that, but I can't remember it.

It nags at me all morning as I go over reports. No news on Jenny Drake. I have to set her file aside. *One for sorrow.* There are fresh problems pushing their way in. The morning news is starting to move on, too. They give a brief blip on Jenny and then go on to the latest political scandal and a local kid killed in a car accident. Hit and run. Some guy blasted through a stop sign in a white car—maybe a Toyota—hit the family on the way back from a soccer game, and sped off again, nowhere to be found. No witnesses. Like the guy materialized long enough to smash into the car and vanished again. So random. So pointless.

Hernandez walks past me, bringing the scent of coffee and cinnamon. She pauses next to my desk to watch the news and shakes her head.

"I hate it when it's kids." Her voice is so quiet, I'm not sure if she's talking to me or herself.

I nod. *One for sorrow.*

She touches my computer monitor, almost like she's catching her balance. Her fingernails are short, carefully filed, but the usually perfect red paint is chipped.

"There's a special place in hell for bastards like that driver." This time she meets my eyes. Her pupils are dilated into vulnerable pools of black.

"Yeah." Though I can't decide if I believe in hell.

"I wish..." She squeezes her eyes shut, takes an uneven

breath. "I wish there was more we could do, but no matter how hard I work, it never ends."

I stand. I want to hold her, but we're in the middle of the station. I have to do something, so I take a chance I haven't before. "Do you need a break? We could grab some lunch. Um, together."

She smiles sadly. "I don't have much of an appetite today. Another time, though. Really." The vague promise rescues my plummeting hopes, and my ego. "And, John? Thanks." She touches my arm and moves on, but the scent of cinnamon lingers. *Two for joy.*

Alone on my lunch break, I Google the nursery rhyme. There it is: One for sorrow, two for joy, three for a girl, four for a boy, five for silver, six for gold, seven for a secret never to be told.

Meaningless. I'd like to hope the three birds mean we're going to find Jenny, but her time is up. I have to file her case with my other frustrations and focus on those I can actually help.

There are a whole flock of magpies outside when I leave. Six of them. Six for gold? I shake my head and drive away.

———

Two weeks later, the official search for Jenny is called off. Some of her family lingers like the ghosts of the case, working with a few stalwart community volunteers who want to help them find closure. Closure. They may find some remains, if they're lucky, but they're never going to find answers.

Hernandez is on leave. "Personal reasons." She needed the break, but the station feels louder and emptier at the same time.

I pull up Jenny's Facebook page again on my break and scroll past pictures of her kids and meals at nice restaurants. An occasional political post. What was she hiding? What was bubbling beneath the smooth surface?

And there it is, buried between a picture of pad thai and a gif of a cat falling into a laundry basket in an endless cycle.

One of those days at work. It never ends. Someone please get me a drink and a tropical beach.

A few hearts and sad-face emojis from friends follow it up, but then there's the cat and the laundry basket with forty thumbs and laughing yellow faces, and we all move on.

Except, Jenny didn't.

The cat falls, reappears on the counter, falls again. And Jenny has another day at work. And another, and another. It never ends. Until it does. I click on the sad-face response. Then I share the cat and its laundry basket. A last tribute before I get back to work.

The magpies have taken a liking to our parking lot. I ignore them.

When I show up the next morning, the chief calls us into the meeting room. He looks...bad. I know that look. He's been up all night, worried about something. His own Jenny Blake is haunting him, making him live on coffee and energy drinks because he can't afford to sleep.

"I have some news about Officer Hernandez," he says.

The room goes still. I saw Hernandez two days ago. She was healthy, whole, beautiful. There were no officer-related shootings overnight. No fatal car accidents.

"Some of you may have heard rumors, but I want you to get the story from me." He takes a long breath. The whole world waits on that breath. "Officer Hernandez died last night. Opioid overdose."

And the world collapses, brittle pieces falling around me, blinding me. It's not possible. We see what drugs do to people every day. How could she have? Hot flares of disbelief, anger, helplessness. Fear.

"It started with a legal prescription. She just...let it get out of hand."

How? How? How?

How did she let it get out of hand? Where was that one moment where she could have turned it around? Did she know, when she popped that pill into her mouth, that it was the moment she was letting go? How did it feel? How did we miss the signs? Depression, dilated pupils, shakiness, restlessness. How did *I* miss the signs?

The chief rambles on about funeral services and grief counselors. It buzzes around me, something from another world, another lifetime. A reality that ended when he said that Hernandez was gone. I swear I can still smell cinnamon.

I make it through the day, but leave a few minutes early. Three magpies sit on the roof of my car. I shoo them away, but they won't leave. They tilt their heads, fix me with black eyes. I swat at them, but they flap and land a little out of reach. I half climb onto my car, trying to get rid of them. One bird hops closer and croaks, "John."

I jump back, hand on my gun. But it must have been my imagination. I know crows can imitate human sounds. Maybe magpies can, too. But what are the chances of them knowing how to imitate my name?

I climb into the car and slam the door. The damn birds can sit there for the whole drive home for all I care. Of course, when I do arrive home, they're gone. No way birds can cling to a car.

"John."

"John."

"John."

Three magpies, sitting in the tree in my yard. I feel sick. I fumble for my keys. It takes two tries to get the key in the lock, hurry inside, close the door on the birds and deadbolt it.

I laugh at myself. A deadbolt for birds? They're not coming inside. Besides, magpies are everywhere, and they're flocking birds. Aren't they?

I hate myself for it, but I Google magpies again. Intelligent, they recognize themselves in the mirror and are expert thieves. They're members of the crow family, and, like crows, flocks can be called a murder, a charm, or a tiding. But they tend to live in pairs, not large groups. There are more references to the nursery rhyme, too. Another, older version, its roots obscured by time: One for sorrow, two for joy, three for a funeral, four for a birth. Five for heaven, six for hell, seven for the devil, his own self.

Three for a funeral.

I shut the browser, turn off the computer. The curtains are closed, but I peek outside. The three birds are still sitting there. Even through the glass, I can hear them.

"John. John. John."

I turn up the TV—loud—and fall asleep in front of it.

———

I'm behind on my paperwork, and I can't focus on the latest burglary. I still smell cinnamon, see Hernandez out of the corner of my eye. The chief calls me into his office to talk.

"There's nothing you could have done about it," he says. "Do you need some time off?"

I take a deep breath. "No. I need to keep working." I have to get myself back under control, back to normal.

But the magpies won't leave me alone.

There are seven of them now. Seven magpies everywhere I go. They caw, "John, John, John." No one else hears it. It's like they're trying to tell me something. Messengers. Crows and ravens were believed to be messengers from the dead. I can't get Hernandez out of my mind. Or Jenny Blake. I dream about them—Hernandez and Blake—staring at me with hollow, black eyes, like they're waiting for something.

It never ends, Jenny Blake tells me, though her mouth is stitched shut.

It's stupid. I'm being paranoid. But I look again at the security footage of Jenny Drake. Zoom in on the power line. Seven. Seven birds with white wings watch as she turns her back on the world.

––––––

The chief gently obliges me to take some time off. I have plenty of paid time I can use. But what am I supposed to do with it? I search the desert, looking for any trace of Jenny Blake. There's nothing. It's so empty. I can look it up on Google maps, and we have aerial photos of every mile of it. But we don't really know it. The desert. Nature. It surrounds us, and we think we've conquered it, but it keeps its secrets.

I end up in my backyard, staring off across that unknowable horizon.

"John." The familiar croak sounds from behind me. I don't have to look to know how many there are, but I turn anyway.

Seven magpies. Seven for a secret never to be told. Or, seven for the devil. Which is it? Is there a difference?

"John," a magpie calls again. The first one. Sorrow.

"John," squawks the second, and I smell cinnamon. Hernandez.

"John." Ringing deep like a funeral bell.

"John." This one is smaller, its voice shrill.

"John." The soothing tones of a preacher, beckoning me back.

"John." A low croak that pierces my soul.

Misery, love, death, life, heaven, hell. All things that touch me, but I can't touch them back. I can't do anything about them. It never ends.

"John," the last magpie speaks, a rasping, graveyard voice. Jenny Blake.

I glance across the desert. The answers are out there somewhere with Blake, Hernandez, and all the others. What do they know that I don't?

I can find out.

"John." Carried like a whisper on the hot desert wind.

It's time to give in. To admit I'm not in control of any of it. To let the facade crumble.

I take off my hat and sunglasses. The desert sun curls around me. Dry heat fills my lungs, burning away the tightness in my chest. Peace. How long has it been since I felt peace?

Somewhere, in the distance, my cell phone rings. Calling me back into the world of questions and uncertainties. But the desert stretches away in front of me, and its secrets beckon.

4

Contrast in White

Isaac Timm

ROGER FLIPPED DISTRACTEDLY through the dog-eared nudie magazine, more out of habit than interest in the air-brushed vixens. Their come-hither stares held no allure under layers of greasy thumb prints. Roger laughed out loud when he flipped to a photo of a haughty, busty blonde who'd had a crude mustache and eye-patch scrawled on her face. The artist had strategically blacked up a few of the centerfold's teeth.

A little bubble over her head read, "Ye get this booty when ye gets the gold. Aarrrgh!"

Roger smiled. It was his wife Helen's handiwork. She came in on weekends to help him square away the service station's books. A brash rancher's daughter, Helen was not bothered by men's magazines. Still, she never missed an opportunity to poke a little fun at readers of smut.

A sudden rush of freezing air and the clattering of the bell above the door made Roger jump. Not out of shame for being caught thumbing the magazine, but because he hadn't heard a car pull into his service station. He tucked the magazine under the counter and sized up the young man who brought the west desert wind into his office.

The fellow was about nineteen or twenty, so skinny the thin leather jacket with racing stripes seemed to be draped on a wire hanger. He wore one of those crudely knitted Peruvian beanie caps popular with college students. His black hair spiked out from under the beanie, oily and clumped, and his watery blue eyes jumped from side to side. He wore grey cargo pants covered with white alkali mud. There were also patches of scabby mud smeared on his long, emaciated face.

Roger smiled. That's why the young man was without a car. He had clearly bogged daddy's car into the salt flat outside of town. Every once in a while, these city kids would plow into the salt flat with dreams of racing on the Bonneville speedway only to find themselves nose-down in a salt bog. He almost felt sorry for them.

The boy mumbled something, and Roger leaned in to hear what seemed to be a sheepish question. The young man's stench almost knocked Roger out, a hybrid of B.O., shit, and rotten meat.

"The father hears. Find the pattern," the boy mumbled.

Then he ignored Roger and rifled frantically through the maps kept at the counter by the checkstand.

Roger's first instinct was to grab the young man by the collar and hoist him bodily out the door. But the young man's glassy, empty eyes made Roger pause. This boy was a meth head, and Roger had dealt with enough of them to know how dangerous and unstable they could become. He would have to talk this boy out of his store and call Sheriff Holston.

"Can I help you?"

The young man continued mumbling to himself.

"Is there anything I can help you find, son?"

The boy's blank, unfocused eyes landed on Roger's face like a fly.

"I am not the son. Only the father chooses the son. He sleeps."

The tweaker made a giggling, gurgling sound, and then stated flatly, "I am the messenger."

With that, the boy reached his hand into his badly stained jacket, pulled out a black book, and slapped it on the counter.

It only took Roger a second to recognize the book. He lived fifteen minutes from the Utah border, and he knew a *Book of Mormon* when he saw it.

Now, Roger had nothing against Mormons. Hell, his hunting buddy was the local bishop. But crystal meth and religion were a toxic mix. He had to reach down inside himself to pull out a calm response.

"Ah, another testament of Christ. What's your favorite passage, son?"

"I'm not the son," restated the young man with another disturbing series of phlegmy gurgles. "His children left with the bloody waters, before—"

The boy's eyes seemed to lose focus for a while. No, Roger thought. Something moved behind them.

"Before, they were abandoned to writher blindly in the dust." The boy began to quiver as if in ecstasy. His throat vibrated, creating an odd buzzing sound as he built to another outburst of fervor.

"But he wakes! Behold."

Even at that distance, it was clear that the smell of rancid meat came from his toothless mouth.

The boy flipped open his *Book of Mormon*. The pages were highlighted, but not over the words. The green and orange neon scribbles were animated, moving in eddies and whorls.

They were hieroglyphs, rising from the page in three dimen-
sions. But the lines formed a pattern, a pattern Roger ached to
understand, but they remained outside his grasp. Roger
thought of the Carl Sagan TV special he had seen as a kid. After
watching it, he hadn't been able to look up at the sky for weeks.
"Billions and billions." The vast void of stars that threatened to
pop the earth and all the beings on it like a pimple. The pattern
was under this void, its foundation, a horror weaving in the
abyss behind the Milky Way.

As Roger stood frozen, trying to find reason in the pattern—
or trying to escape it—a clammy hand touched his. The boy's
fingers were covered with some kind of mucous. It burned
Roger, and when the boy pulled his hand back, part of Roger's
skin came away with it, stretching like candle wax.

An unspeakable terror gripped him.

Roger had not noticed the large lug wrench the boy had
taken from the wall. He was transfixed by the pattern, by his
bloody torn hand. The boy smashed in Roger's skull.

———

The messenger cocked its head as blood from the mechanic's
head poured over the counter. The corpse didn't matter. The
messenger was transfixed by the blood. Yes, the pattern! The
sign! Father was waking. The messenger traced its fingers
through the blood. Outside, the wind blew streaks of snow
from the salt pan into drifts that formed against the blacktop.
The messenger briefly noted the contrast in white.

5

Hunger

E.B. Wheeler

MOST OF THE lights were off in Abuela's little bungalow when I arrived. Why do old people like to sit in the dark? I balanced the grocery sacks while digging in my purse for the key to the front door. My finger hooked the ring, but when I pulled it out, I fumbled it. It fell to the cement with a metallic ping. I groaned and set down the bags to get the key. When I stuck it in the deadbolt and turned it, I found that the door had been unlocked all along.

"Oh, Abuela!" I said under my breath, gathering the sacks again.

The door groaned when I pushed it open. I flipped the hall light switch, but nothing happened. Burned out. Another thing on my to-do list.

"Charo, is that you?" Abuela Rosario called from the living room.

I dropped my keys onto the dining room table with a clunk and hurried into the dark kitchen to put the groceries away. I was surprised Abuela heard me over the TV. At least her ears were still good.

I clicked on the lights. They were the old fluorescent tube type, and one of them buzzed and flickered before settling into "on." The kitchen still seemed too dark. Time to get those changed, too.

"Charo?" Abuela's voice cracked.

I shut the fridge door firmly on the milk and cheese and rolled my tight shoulders. Here we go.

"It's not Charo," I called. "It's Laura. Your granddaughter."

Some days, Abuela remembered.

Silence answered me, though. That was new. I put the cereal away, casting a quick glance at the old gas stove. Baby locks hugged each knob. Abuela would not be trying to cook again. I hadn't been able to get all the smoke stains off the ceiling from last time. But there was plenty of bran cereal with raisins— Abuela's favorite—plus bananas, yogurt, and other things that didn't need to be cooked. I would make a real dinner if Abuela didn't chase me out with a broom.

The sputtering fluorescent tube zapped and went out. I groaned and turned around.

Abuela stood in the kitchen doorway.

I gave a start but quickly regained my composure and smiled. Be patient and cheerful, the doctor had advised me. "Are you hungry, Rosario?"

It had to be "Rosario" and not "Abuela," because if she didn't remember me, "Abuela" made her angry.

She rubbed her arms. A bruise marked her skin with a purple crescent. I spotted another farther up her forearm, faded now to a sickly green. Had she been biting herself? It looked a little small for that. She probably didn't even recall how she did it. A chill of uncertainty settled in my stomach. Maybe it was time to admit she couldn't live alone anymore, but moving her would be upsetting.

"You're not Charo." She watched me with vague, nervous eyes, one of them clouded blue by a cataract. Good luck getting her to see a doctor about that, though.

It was one of the bad days. Most of the days were bad lately.

Stay calm. Redirect. "No, Charo couldn't come today." My mother had died three years earlier. "Would you like soup for dinner?"

"It doesn't work." Abuela scowled at the stove.

"I can fix it. Are you hungry?"

Abuela glanced back at the living room. "Do you have enough for everyone? They're hungry."

"Sure. There's plenty."

Abuela often talked to her dead husband and sisters—thought they were still around and visiting her. Who knows? Maybe they were. It used to creep me out, but now it was just part of the game, like a child's imaginary friends. I grabbed a pot from the cupboard and took the safety knob off the front burner.

A cold, arthritic hand clutched my arm. "They stole my remote control. They keep changing the channel."

"Okay. I'll come help you."

I left the pot and headed for the hallway. Usually, Abuela led the way, but today she hung back. The dark hallway creaked, and I thought I saw a shadow move in the living room. My breath caught, and cold sweat broke out over my skin. The door had been unlocked. Had someone broken in?

I grabbed a stick umbrella from the hallway stand and snuck down the dim corridor. A woman screamed from the living room. I jumped and tightened my grip on the umbrella. Just the TV. I peeked into the living room.

The TV blasted some old slasher flick, but otherwise the worn couch and chairs looked exactly as they always did—as they had since I was a child, except more faded and threadbare.

"Are they gone?" Abuela asked, padding up behind me on slippered feet.

I let out a tight breath and set the umbrella down. "There's no one here."

The doctor had warned me that Abuela would get more confused. Eventually, she would have to leave the little house she had lived in since she fled Franco's Spain for the US.

Behind us, the other kitchen light blinked out. I glanced over my shoulder. Our shadows stretched back to blend with the darkness of the kitchen.

A bang from the living room made me jump. I looked back to the blue glow of the TV and chuckled, though it sounded strained, even to me. "Abuela, what are you watching?"

"I don't know! They changed the channel. They like to play tricks on me—scare me."

I sighed and dug around the couch, lifting the cushions and tossing the pillows aside, but I couldn't find the remote. Abuela probably put it in the shower or something. I walked up to the TV and changed it back to reruns of Jeopardy. Ken Jennings appeared on the screen, grinning nervously as Alex Trebek introduced a new set of clues.

Abuela still lingered at the entrance to the room.

"They're not happy," she said.

I glanced at the TV. "You want to watch something else?"

"It's the children."

I looked around the room with its worn couch and coffee table stacked with neglected magazines. There were a few photos of my cousins and me as children and more of us growing up. We took turns checking in on her, yet she rarely recognized any of us lately.

"What about the children?" I asked wearily, trying not to let my hurt feelings color my voice.

"The dead children. They won't listen to me."

A shiver crawled up my back. "Dead children?"

The TV crackled, and the slasher film jumped back onto the screen. I slammed the power button off.

"They're so noisy," she whispered. "They keep me awake at night."

Okay. This was getting creepy. But Spain under Franco's dictatorship had been a dark place. Who knows what Abuela had seen there—what memories still haunted her? The doctor told me not to argue with her. Redirect. My stomach felt queasy, but I said, "We should have dinner."

"The children are hungry. They're always hungry."

A wave of goose bumps prickled over me. "Let's get back to the kitchen, then." Turn on some more lights, too.

"They drink our fear, but I don't want to feed them anymore." She crossed herself and muttered a prayer, staring back toward the dark kitchen.

I turned to watch the hallway. The shadows seemed deeper than before. Shivering. Like they were excited. I took a step back. The TV turned on, blasting static. Abuela shrank against the wall.

My mouth went dry. The shadows down the hallway pulsed with a black so deep it hurt my eyes. And pieces of the darkness shaped like children with limbs too thin and sharp broke off to skitter along the walls like emaciated rats.

Abuela whimpered. I screamed.

"Out! Out!" I grabbed Abuela's arm and dragged her into the brightness of the living room.

But the lights dimmed as though a fog had rolled into the room. Singsongy voices chanted a wordless playground song in the corridor. Coming closer.

I pushed Abuela toward the window. She was crying now.

"The children. Please, stop the children!"

I looked back again. Smelled the rotten egg stench of propane. Had I turned the stove on? Had Abuela? Didn't matter.

I shoved the window open. Abuela stared back into the shadows, her eyes unfocused. I hauled her in front of me, forced her to climb out.

The sulfuric reek of propane grew stronger. The lights buzzed, strobing against the darkness. Something sharp pierced my calf. Burning pain radiated from a shadow form twining around my leg, sucking the strength from me. I shrieked, kicked free, scrambled after Abuela into the cool night air.

The hungry shadows roared like an angry tide. I clutched Abuela's hand and ran. The living room lights popped out behind us, leaving the patchy lawn in darkness.

An explosion shook the air and threw us to the ground. Shards of glass and wood rained down on us, and heat rolled over my skin. My ears rang, but I thought I heard angry shrieks under the whoosh of the flames jumping into the night sky.

Then everything went still.

Abuela looked at me. "Laura?" Her voice sounded clearer, stronger. "What happened?"

"There was a fire, Abuela." I looked back at the bright blaze crackling in the skeleton of the house. "But you're safe now."

6

Fedora Man

Mike Nelson

IT BEGAN for me on a pleasant but sad fall evening in my local cemetery, though I suppose the real beginning goes back much further. I had recently lost my wife and went to the cemetery often to feel her presence. Before she died, I had been diagnosed as pre-diabetic and told that diet and exercise were the first steps in getting my health under control. Because I have bad knees, I couldn't jog without discomfort, and I'm old enough that exerting myself in a gym might create even more severe issues. I decided that walking would be the perfect exercise.

My first experiences with walking were not happy. First, dogs in my neighborhood didn't seem to like me much, and being an animal lover, I couldn't force myself to carry doggie mace or ammonia in a water pistol to keep from being bitten. Plus, the sidewalks in my part of town were often rough and uneven and overgrown with low-hanging vegetation, if they existed at all.

One evening while I was visiting the grave of my dearly

departed wife, Margie, I noticed a sign prohibiting dogs or glass in the cemetery. I decided that I would do my walking there. My preferred time was just before sundown when most sane folks had already gone home to their families, leaving the grounds quiet, unharried, and uncluttered.

The more I walked, the more I enjoyed it, and the better I felt. I cherished my time away from the telephone, the television, and the interruptions by well-meaning neighbors dropping by to offer their condolences. Last, but certainly not least, I needed to escape the constant reminders that filled the home I had shared with my spouse of fifty-three years. All it took was a quick glance at a family photo to bring back my grief.

I'm a regimented sort of person, so I always started my walks at the same time every evening. As the days grew shorter that fall, I soon found myself completing the last lap in almost total darkness.

It was on one such evening that I sensed it for the first time. I didn't hear or see anything unusual, but I had a distinct feeling that someone was watching me. I didn't let it bother me much that first night, but when the same thing happened the next night, I started carrying an LED flashlight that could cast a blinding beam of light at least half a block.

The first few nights, the flashlight gave me confidence. When I got that uneasy sensation, I'd flash my light at the headstones and off through the trees and bushes, looking for whoever was following me. I saw nothing, but the eerie feeling that I was being watched lingered.

Unable to shrug it off, I adjusted my regimen, making sure I arrived at my locked car before the street lights flickered on in the evening. Still, I felt unseen eyes on my back.

I quit walking in the cemetery for a while, opting instead to walk first thing in the morning in a newer neighborhood where the sidewalks were better. That worked until someone let their dog out to do his business just as I walked by. I ended up on the hood of the man's car, yelling at his snarling dog until he heard the ruckus and came to my rescue. He was not at all amused by the dent I left in the hood of his car but agreed not to press charges when I threatened to call the animal control officer to pick up his vicious dog.

The next evening, I traveled back to the cemetery, and that's the first time I actually saw him.

I was on my last lap, the sun had set, and I was on the home stretch to my parked car when I felt his presence. I noticed a figure leaning against a pine tree in the deep shadows. It was too dim to see him clearly. All I really remember that first time was that he was dressed from head-to-foot in dark clothing and was wearing an old-fashioned fedora.

A cold sensation crept over me. I don't know why I was so intimidated. He wasn't following me, and he didn't do anything threatening. He just stood there—watching.

On the way home, I tried to rationalize what I'd seen. Surely there were other lonely people in the world—someone like myself who was so overcome by grief that he didn't want to reopen still-raw wounds by hanging around the house. The only difference was, he was simply watching, not walking, and he was never in the same place twice. I needed peace and space, and in reality, I needed to feel some closeness to Margie. Visiting her grave did that.

He wasn't there the rest of the week, and I pushed my anxiety to the back of my mind, convinced that the dark figure was simply another lonely man like myself.

Monday night, he was back.

He still watched me from the shadows, standing far off, just beyond where I might recognize him and yet in full view as if to let me know he was there. I didn't actually observe him following me, yet I saw him several times in different places as I walked my laps. He was always on the periphery, always watching, but never approaching. He certainly had the right to be there, but his presence troubled me.

I decided to talk to a policeman friend of mine about the stranger.

He just laughed. "This city is full of weirdos. If you're concerned about it, you shouldn't walk there that time of night."

I *was* concerned, but I refused to be intimidated by this peeper. In case he decided to do more than watch, I bought a can of pepper spray. I had a concealed-carry permit for a firearm but was so unsure of my marksmanship, especially in the gloom, that I was afraid I might put a bullet through the walls of any of the dozens of homes surrounding the graveyard.

I tried a show of bravado, striding around my regular route as if I owned the cemetery and feared no one. The dark figure only became bolder. Instead of slinking around the dark perimeters, he watched me while standing in the shadows alongside trees in the middle of the cemetery—and he moved closer every day. Try as I might, I never actually caught him moving from one location to another.

Unnerved, I altered my routine. Some days I'd walk after lunch. Other days I'd walk after breakfast. Still other days I'd walk after dinner in the evening. It made no difference what time of day I went there. He was always there. I didn't actually see him during broad daylight, but I could feel him—watching. Did he ever go home?

I bought a small rear-view mirror for my eyeglasses like I'd seen bicyclists wear to watch the traffic approaching from behind. That evening, I spotted him standing in the shadows under the spreading branches of a horse chestnut tree. The leaves had turned their yellowish-orange fall colors, and a few had started to fall, but the rest still shaded the ground beneath the tree. I carefully watched him in the mirror as I strode on. One moment he was standing under the chestnut tree, and the next, he was standing in the heavy shadows beneath a fir tree some hundred or more paces farther on. His dark legs did not move.

No mortal could move like that, and I wanted no part of whatever game he was playing. Until that moment, I was convinced, like my cop friend, that he was just one of the many weirdos stalking our city. If he was a spirit roaming the confines of the cemetery, though, I would respect his boundaries and leave him alone in it.

I took to walking Main Street in broad daylight, hoping to put the phantom behind me. Yet even though I couldn't see him anymore, I still felt his icy presence. Watching.

Convinced I was courting insanity, I tried to ignore the feelings. I rationalized that if I couldn't see him, he didn't exist. The feelings were only there when I was out walking.

Then that changed, too.

One beautiful Sunday evening, I carried my dinner out onto the back patio. I had planned on soaking up some of the crisp autumn air and watching the leaves fall while I ate.

He stood under my apple tree at the back of the yard.

I dropped my plate, swept back inside, grabbed a fireplace poker, and raced back out to the deck.

He was gone.

I double-checked all my doors and windows that night before I went to bed to be sure they were all locked. I slept with the fireplace poker.

Morning found me lying crossways on my bed, clutching the poker. I felt like I hadn't slept a wink.

I needed answers, so I sought out my pastor. Margie and I hadn't been the most stellar attendees to his weekly services, and the pastor spent a good share of our hour together getting reacquainted rather than addressing my problem.

In the end, he had no answers. He spoke in rambling generalities of life after death and spirits.

Then he looked me in the eye. "Did this... entity ever attempt to communicate with or... or control you?"

"No. I wondered if Margie might have a message for me, but she wouldn't send a stranger. Especially not one who makes me feel so uneasy."

He drew a deep breath of relief and let it out. "Another thing you could consider. I have a friend you could talk to. A psychologist."

He handed me a card.

I came away seriously wondering if I was losing my mind. I felt sane, but what does sanity really feel like? Did I need another opinion?

I walked in the cemetery that afternoon, blatantly tempting the man in the fedora to appear. He didn't, and I had a pleasant creep-free experience. By the time I got home, I had decided that what I was seeing and feeling was a figment of my imagination. But that frightened me even more. What if losing Margie had broken something inside me?

I called my pastor's buddy, Doctor Spainhower.

The doctor's assistant took my call, listened impatiently to my heart-felt ravings for a few moments, and then stopped me and set up an appointment with the doctor for the following afternoon.

My first hour with Dr. Bryant Spainhower was productive

enough. He was soft-spoken, professional, and very attentive. The problem was, all he did was listen. By the end of our first session, I felt like he knew and perhaps understood my situation, but he offered no solution other than a follow-up appointment two days hence. My visit left me even more anxious. I didn't want to accept that I might be losing my mind.

I went to the cemetery that evening. I needed to feel the peace Margie's gravesite offered me.

I didn't walk my usual route. I drove straight to Margie's burial plot, walked to her grave, and sat on the grass, staring at the words I'd had engraved on her headstone.

Then I felt him.

His presence sent shivers down my spine. At first, I didn't dare look up. When I did, he was standing in the shadows of a mostly leafless mulberry tree less than twenty feet away. I didn't see his eyes or his face—only the fedora.

Excruciating pain and blind panic overwhelmed me. Then I felt nothing.

I was lying on my back when I woke up. It was dark, and I was chilled to the bone.

Panic-stricken, I struggled to my feet and looked around. Fedora Man was gone, but his presence wasn't. I spun around to look for my car. It was still there, but it was pointed in the wrong direction. I know I hadn't left it parked facing that way, sitting directly beneath a one-way street sign. I've always been a conscientious driver. I felt in my right-hand pants pockets for my car keys. They weren't there. My panic deepened. I fumbled for my cell phone. It wasn't in my shirt pocket where I'd left it, but as I searched through the rest of my clothing, I found it in my left-hand pants pocket—along with my car keys.

Every muscle in my body ached. Although I found it hard to move, I struggled to my car, locked myself inside, and sat shivering as the engine warmed. I sat behind the wheel for a long time after that before I had enough strength and control to drive home.

Inside my house, I locked the doors behind me, drew a hot bath, and locked the bathroom door—something I hadn't done in the fifty-three years I'd lived with Margie—and eased into the scalding water.

My mind ran rampant while I lay there, trying to decide if I'd had a mental lapse or if there was something much more sinister to my evening's experience. My thoughts locked on my car keys. I had always been a creature of habit. My car keys belonged in my right-hand pocket, my wallet in my left rear pocket, my cell phone in my left-hand shirt pocket. I never put my phone in my pants pockets for fear I'd break the screen.

Then another thought rang through my fumbling mind. What if Fedora Man were left-handed? That would explain—

I couldn't even finish the idea. Had he taken possession of my body? What had he made me do? Had he used my phone or my credit cards?

Waves of fear swept over me. Was that even possible? Why me? Would God allow that? What did Fedora Man want with me? How far would it go? What could I do to stop him?

My next appointment with Dr. Spainhower couldn't come soon enough. I was convinced by then that Fedora Man was real. If he wasn't, I was indeed losing my mind.

Bryant listened patiently to my new stories. This time, however, I noticed a slight change in his demeanor. Where he'd sat stone-faced before, now I spotted an occasional eyebrow lift. He stopped me on several different occasions to ask in-depth questions. He seemed to be especially interested when I mentioned my car keys, cell phone, and the improperly parked car.

Just as I thought we were making progress, a soft chime announced the end of our hour-long session, and he stood and excused himself for a moment. When he returned, he handed me a tiny bottle full of pills to help me cope until we could meet again—two days hence.

The pills—to be taken first thing in the morning and again at night—had an interesting effect on my consciousness. I was much more relaxed. But Fedora Man was waiting for me beneath my apple tree just after dinner that evening.

The horror and pain I felt when he closed in on me were the same.

This time when I woke up, I was lying face-down on my couch in the living room, and my car keys, wallet, and cell phone were grouped neatly together on the coffee table—almost as if the entity had been listening in Dr. Spainhower's office when I spilled my guts. Was the man ever-present, only seen when he wanted me to see him?

Feeling the need to get clean, I took my evening pill, filled the tub with water, and shed my clothes. When I faced the mirror over the bathroom vanity, I noticed the mark on my neck. I hadn't had a hickey since high school, and yet there it stood: large, unmistakable, and embarrassing. I obviously couldn't give myself a hickey. This wasn't something that a pinch could have caused, and it wasn't a bruise.

Frenzied thoughts raced through my confused mind as I tried to relax in my bath. If he was using my body as his own, how could I stop him? I thought about using handcuffs, but he would know where I hid the key. Maybe I could swallow the key, but how would I free myself when I was "myself?" If I set up a video camera in my house, he'd know how to turn it off. If I asked a neighbor to watch for me, I would sound totally insane.

What could my neighbor tell me—that I came out of my house and went somewhere in my car?

I needed someone I could trust—someone who would believe what I was telling them. I had nobody. Both of my sons lived out-of-state. Margie and I had been each other's "everything" for so long we had no close friends. I played golf with some friends twice a month, but they'd simply be convinced that I'd lost my mind. The only other person I'd drawn into my circle of confidence was Dr. Spainhower, and I was convinced he already had a stereotyped answer for who I was, or what I had become.

I spent a restless night, took my morning pill about ten when I finally forced myself out of bed, showered, and went downtown for lunch.

My regular eatery was packed, and I wasn't in the mood for a half-hour wait, so I got back in my car and drove randomly down the boulevard until a sign for a diner I'd never visited before caught my eye. I was delighted that I didn't have to wait to be served, but—

An attractive middle-aged waitress I didn't know, whose name was Francis—by the name-tag over her left breast— seemed overly-eager to seat me. It didn't take an Einstein to realize she knew me by the way she hovered around me. That's when I spotted the mark on her neck. She had a love bite that nearly matched mine.

She brought me a cup of coffee and an appetizer. "Here it is. Your favorite."

I don't drink coffee, and the favorite she brought me was disgusting.

"I'm not feeling well," I told her. "Can I get the check?"

She scrawled her phone number on my copy of the receipt. As she refilled my water, she whispered. "I'll be off at eight."

When I got home and picked up the mail, I had a traffic ticket summons waiting for me among the usual bills. Even though the officer's handwriting was barely legible, I could discern the date, time, place, driver's license, license plate numbers, and a description of the infraction. I had been ticketed for driving ninety miles per hour in a seventy zone near some mile marker on the freeway. The signature scribbled on the promise-to-appear portion of the ticket was completely foreign to me. The signature's letters were slanted the wrong direction. I read the date and time. I'd been ticketed while lying unconscious in the cemetery.

Now, maybe, I had proof for Dr. Spainhower. I almost said the words aloud then realized that I might not be alone, so I kept my comments to myself.

I could hardly wait for my one o'clock appointment the next afternoon. Believing that Fedora Man couldn't read my thoughts, I did nothing out-of-the-ordinary that might tip my hand, but I was ready for the doctor the moment he closed the office door behind us.

I ignored the doctor's salutations, speaking rapidly but succinctly and getting right down to business. I needed answers. I needed a cure, and I needed it now.

Bryant tried to interrupt a time or two but finally sat back, made notes, and let me rant. He didn't take much notice until I showed him the two pieces of physical evidence. The love bite didn't interest him much, but the signature on the traffic ticket did. That's when I felt Fedora Man's presence as strong as I'd ever felt it in the cemetery, and by the look on his face, Bryant was feeling him, too.

He took the ticket—with his left hand—and studied it for a moment before pulling a piece of scratch paper from his desk. Then he tried to emulate my signature using his left hand. The loops and swirls nearly matched the signature on the ticket. He looked me in the eyes, opened his notebook, and turned back to the notes he'd taken during our first session—the ones where I'd mentioned finding my keys and phone in the wrong pocket.

The color drained from his face, leaving his skin pallid and moist. Without another word, he picked up his telephone. I caught some of his side of the conversation, but he spoke so softly and rapidly, I didn't understand much. As he ended the call, he turned his undivided attention back to me.

He made small talk for the next few minutes. I guessed he knew Fedora Man was in the room, and he didn't want to tip his hand.

I jumped when two men dressed in white smocks knocked on the office door and then entered without waiting for Dr. Spainhower to answer, yet somehow I wasn't surprised.

Moments later, I was speeding through traffic in a nondescript van with Bryant and the two men dressed in white. When I tried to ask a question, Dr. Spainhower lifted his index finger to his lips. I felt Fedora Man's presence and understood.

Bryant didn't offer me any medication, and the two men in the back of the van with me did not attempt to restrain me.

The drive to "the facility" took about thirty minutes. That was the first time the two men in white touched me, and even then, they only lightly held my elbows to escort me into the building.

Dr. Spainhower stopped at the reception desk while the other two whisked me down a long hallway to a padded room without furniture or windows. There they asked me to completely disrobe and offered me a one-piece, short-sleeved jump-suit in exchange. When I attempted to talk, one or the other simply held a single finger to their lips.

Then without another word, the two left me alone in the

room.

Slow minutes ticked away. I trusted that Bryant knew what to do.

Finally, my doctor's soft voice came over a speaker set high on the wall above the door. He apologized for not believing my story and explained.

"Fedora Man, as he manifests to you, is indeed real, and he's dangerous. Once he grooms someone, he won't leave them until he's ruined them. By keeping you in here, we can prevent that."

The intensity of Fedora Man's presence tripled. The now all-too-familiar pain and fear swept over me, and then I felt nothing.

Sometime later, I became aware of others in the room with me. I was lying on my back, restrained to a bed, and an I.V. at my bedside dripped transparent fluid into my left arm.

Dr. Spainhower was speaking.

"... three weeks. It took that long to get 'Fedora Man' to release his hold on you."

"He took over when I lost consciousness?" I asked.

"Yes. We have videos we can show you later. When you're stable. Meanwhile, we have you in protective custody. We want to keep you here until we know the entity will leave you alone."

"I have to stay here?" I tried to sit up.

"It will protect you and your interests. Your reputation. Your children. We don't know what the entity will do with your body if you're free."

It was all pretty hard to swallow at first. They wouldn't let my boys see me for fear that Fedora Man would transfer himself to them. They'd done some investigative work, in the meantime, to see what had happened while I was under *his* influence. They paid my traffic ticket and somehow had my record expunged. They followed leads from my cellphone and credit card and shut down several financial transactions Fedora Man had entered into in my name. They had a chat with the waitress with the monkey bite and treated us both for gonorrhea.

Now, I live a new reality. I can't leave the hospital because they can't control Fedora Man. Dr. Spainhower comes to visit once a week and has shown me other case studies like mine. None of those patients survived. They were all single and male —many had been recently widowed. Fedora Man preyed on them because they had nobody to counteract all the things he did once he had control of their bodies. Once Fedora Man destroyed them financially, emotionally, socially, and physically, they'd take their own lives, and he'd move on to another victim. The doctor didn't know how long Fedora Man had been active, and unfortunately, they didn't have a cure.

I still feel Fedora Man's presence from time to time, but at least he can't use my body to hurt anyone. I live alone in my enclosure, where I have nothing I can use to hurt myself or others.

I miss Margie. Despite what my two sons may think, I'm well. It's been challenging to face the fact that I will never leave here, but I am content in knowing that eventually I'll be free, and then if there is a God—which I believe more and more there must be—He will bring down hellfire and damnation on Fedora Man. When He does, I only hope I can be there to testify of my suffering and see that Fedora Man is sent to the depths of Hell where he can never hurt anyone again.

I did have an unsettling thought the other day, though. Although I'm confined to this institution, Fedora Man is free to come and go as he pleases. I wonder how many others have seen a dark stranger lurking in the shadows and not known, yet, the real danger they're in.

7

Pearls Before Swine

Eric Bishop

WHATEVER IT WAS, my horse wasn't having any.

Ten years of ranch life had taken most of his give-a-damn. The little things that'll spook a rookie, like the quick movement of a rope or the backfire of a car, didn't bother him, but right now, Goliath's ears were cocked forward to a place he would not go. Most of the stuff he once thought would kill him hadn't even made him yawn, like the first time he carried a pack-saddle. But horses were particular. Sometimes a thing they'd seen a hundred times would scare the bejesus right out of them.

"That blanket's possessed," we'd joke as the horse went berserk. "Never was before, but it is right now."

The year I broke Goliath, a river swept a stick-carrying beaver between his legs. Goliath went bull-goose looney and bucked his way back to the bank while I wished for a bar of soap. And there he was, reins dangling and snorting at the beaver who just kept swimming to wherever it had in mind for the stick. Then, seeing me with my boots sloshing and river dripping from my soaked hat spooked Goliath again.

There'd been lots of trails since, but right now he just wouldn't go. I didn't think much of it. Perhaps the waning light or the wind or the dark clouds were chock-full of demons only he could see. I was just glad to be in a place I didn't have to wear a mask or listen to people gripe about politics or some other damned thing. I spurred Goliath, but all he would do is back up, snort, then strike with his front hooves.

So, I swung down and tied him to an arrow-straight pine then looked toward a pile of boulders with raspberry thicket covering the top. It rustled, probably from a black bear. And sure enough, Goliath snorted his wish to be in Hell and Gone. But a gunshot would scare the bear away, and a hatful of fresh raspberries would sure beat the jerky and crackers in my saddlebags.

I tried to quiet him. "Whoa, whoa! Nothin's gonna eat you."

Not convinced, Goliath brushed me aside with the toss of his head then kicked with his hind legs. His ears and eyes focused on the boulders and the shaking in the bushes. Then he went to pulling back hard enough to shake pinecones free, which scared him more. For a moment, I wondered if he'd topple the tree, but it held and so did my knot.

"Not gonna be easy to get that undone," I grumbled.

A hiss and then a squeal came from behind. I spun back toward the raspberries and for the first time thought this might not be a bear having dinner. I tried to slide my Winchester from the scabbard but Goliath spun into me. The hiss came again. Between two boulders next to the thicket was fur. It looked matted with mud, so I doubted it was living. I hadn't seen it from the saddle, but the change in angle from saddleback to feet could account for that. So I palmed my six-shooter and walked.

A grouse exploded at my feet, his wings taking my heartbeat to an overhead branch.

When I looked again, the fur was gone.

Whatever it was should leave tracks, but there wasn't a single track or berry. Smeared mud, warm to my touch and still damp, marked the boulders where I'd spotted the fur.

Then a lightning strike lit the sky, answered by booming thunder.

Something big was running away. Goliath.

"Git back here!" I yelled, but he galloped, clipping trees and breaking branches. I spun, scanning until my eyes rested on the tree where Goliath had been tied, but no lead-rope.

Someone with a thumb stronger than mine had to have untied that knot—or cut the rope. And that same thumb might now be wrapped around my Winchester.

I dropped behind the bushes. More lightning and thunder, then rain started, but I lay still as thimble-sized drops soaked my shirt. It built to a downpour and ran down my neck. If the trigger of my own gun was going to be pulled on me, I wasn't going to give the shooter a daytime target. That was the plan, to wait for dark. The wind started, and soon I was clenching my jaw to stop the chattering.

My stomach told me it was past dinnertime. Oh, for the jerky in my saddlebags. Or the cell phone. I'd wanted to get away from the noise of social media, but now I was really cut off.

The rain slowed, quit, but came again as the sun set. Then things went pitch black with random lightning. Each time I looked at a different spot to study how best to make my run, but there was never enough time. Did I see a tree, a rock, or something else? And then I'd hear noises from that direction or from behind. The lightning would crack again, and the instant of seeing was never what I remembered. Then a crackling spilled from east to west and dammit if there wasn't a man standing twenty feet way. He was covered in pelts, but when the woods lit up again, it was a broken tree trunk. Then the lightning quit, and wind rubbed tree trunks against each other.

Eventually, the moon came up and cast enough light to see. Stay longer and my legs would be too stiff for running, so I picked out a Douglas fir big enough for hiding at my eleven. If no bullets came, and I made it, I'd pick the next spot.

I ran, six-shooter in hand, but something between me and the moon veered toward me. I juked, ran blind until my lungs gave out. The six-shooter lighter, my feet like bricks, I cocked the hammer, spun, and stopped, my ragged breath a map to find me. Whatever it was must have stopped when I did, but I saw and heard nothing. I held my breath for a half minute, hoping to hear it breathe.

Movement between the trees gave me a target.

Boom.

My ears rang. Something behind me moved, so I spun then shot rounds two and three.

I tasted a granite rock but stayed on my feet with blood spilling from my spit lips over my chin. The next rock glanced off my shoulder and I spun to shoot rounds four, five, and six into a moving shadow. Without looking away, I worked a bullet from my belt loop while thumbing open the revolver's trap door. I dropped the bullet in the cylinder, but it sprang from the ground, blunt force knocking the gun away, and it was already at my neck.

I thrashed tooth and fingernail against something a foot taller than my six feet. Sticks cracked under foot as I tried for my knife, but a hand closed around my forearm. The bones in my wrist popped like match sticks, and my fingers went numb.

The thing tossed me aside then grabbed my foot and drug me like a calf to be branded. My good hand palmed a rock only to have it torn away as easy as candy from a baby. A blow to my chest took my wind. Then it hit me in the head, and I was a fish on the beach until the lighter places blended with the dark.

I woke with blood still oozing down my face and chest. I rolled to an elbow but quit and looked at the stars. My knife, scabbard, and belt were gone. I spent the next hour too hurt to move, worrying over my lifeless hand.

Warm breath woke me at dawn. I kicked and squirmed, igniting fire in my forearm. It was back to finish me, but then I recognized Goliath's upright ears. The saddle was beneath his belly, the Winchester gone, but my bedroll was still fastened behind the saddle.

Using the horn and rigging for a handle, I pulled myself up and was able to right the saddle with my good arm. The saddlebag was empty—no jerky and no cell phone—but I freed the bedroll, burrowed into the blankets, and shivered myself warm. Sticks cracked, but Goliath stood statue still, unworried by the forest's noises until the sun rose. I made a splint with two branches and felt tingling in my fingers then wrapped it with strips torn form a blanket.

Goliath, God bless him, stood for me to climb aboard.

He walked out easy, perhaps knowing my fight was gone. The morning's first sun cast shadows forcing the night's dew into steam rising like spirits leaving the earth. My swollen lips, scrapes under my torn shirt, and several lumps on my head turned numb as I dozed. We crossed a stream then rounded a bend. My head throbbed again. Air, I needed more, and then I fell.

Goliath was standing over me, his warm breath exhaling against my neck. Something rustled to the left.

I blinked but couldn't clear the fuzz of a shaking bush and horse running away through a tunnel.

"Pearls before swine," I whispered. "It'll be me first to Hell and Gone."

The blows were rocks thrown at a house with me waiting for the walls to crumble. And then I was being dragged, but not over sticks and rocks and branches. I was in a cool running stream which turned warm and became all the air I needed.

8

Lurker: A Novella
TJ Tarbet

DEATH. To leak out the redness that gave life. To stop moving. To be unbound from flesh and from form. Something like that. The Lurker didn't understand it very well.

Murder. To let out the red muck that ran through these creature's bodies. Some of it dripped from his claws. What did these things call it? Blood? Yes, that was it. Blood.

Useful stuff. More useful than the creatures who carried it.

He stepped over a body, shifted one of the appendages that sprang from the core of meat and bone and skin. There. That was right. Not perfect, but he would need to murder another one of these things for that, and there wasn't time to hunt one down.

Time. Another concept invented by these small-minded things, but one that bound him, confused him, constrained him, much like this lanky collection of flesh and bone.

For being so remarkably limited, these human things came up with a number of strange ideas, rules. What was the point of these pitiful creatures, anyway? How were there so very *many* of them? This entire sphere was choked with them. Arrogant, little things. *Death* and *murder* implied something of value had been lost when these little things ceased to move, to breathe.

He heard a metallic squeal and a sudden intake of breath behind him. Another one. How fortunate. More blood, more flesh, more bone.

That, and the creatures made such delightful sounds as they died.

He spun and leapt at the poor, fat creature as it desperately tried to grab the thing at its hip. Delicious terror was plastered on the thing's face. What were these creatures called again? Humans? They must be. Only a race barely capable of independent thought would ever call themselves something so undescriptive.

This one was faster than it looked. By the time the Lurker had landed, the human had already drawn the gleaming thing from its hip.

This was going to be a lot more fun than he'd thought.

The Lurker dove behind the pudgy thing as the weapon in its hand banged. Not fast enough. He spun and lashed out, severing one of the silly thing's legs. A stream of red erupted as it fell, joining the gore of its comrades. The thing in the fat creature's hand banged again as the creature fell, and something pinged lamely in a corner of the building.

Now the real fun started. The Lurker vanished into the shadows as the thing howled. Its screams were succulent; a pleasant tingle ran up the Lurker's spine. But even more entertaining was what it did next. The human took the silly piece of cloth that it wore around its neck and tied it as tightly as it could around its severed leg, pinching off the fountain of warm, sticky essence. The Lurker almost laughed. The pitiful thing thought it was actually going to *survive*.

The Lurker reached out and pushed over a squat metal cylinder. The clang echoed through the chamber. By the time the human had whipped his head around and fired, however, the Lurker was already gone, dashing behind the human, letting the wind stir its hair.

Another shot.

The Lurker laughed, stalking at the edge of the thing's vision.

Bang.

The human was weeping now. Blubbering, in fact. It was almost cute. Fascinating how these pitiful creatures clung to life. Greedy little creatures. Of all the things in the cosmos to be blessed with life, why these small-souled creatures?

Not that life was particularly desirable, the Lurker thought. It felt as though his soul barely fit in this crawling collection of sensation and physicality.

Finally, the Lurker crept into the incandescent puddle the human had drug itself to. The human's eyes widened as he saw the full glory of the Lurker's form. As the Lurker closed in on his prey, the human raised his weapon. It was trembling so violently, the Lurker thought it might shake itself to pieces. Just as the Lurker was about to sink his long, black claws into soft flesh, the human fired.

Something impacted his chest like a meteorite, knocking him back a pace and igniting in the center of his chest like a newborn star. The Lurker threw his head back and howled. He clutched and tore at the new hole in his bosom, shrieking and writhing. He lurched, his screams echoing off the walls, a deafening cacophony. The Lurker stumbled backwards on unsteady legs, seeking the refuge of the darkness.

What had this insolent wretch done to him? It was like a speck of rage sunk into his chest, searing his physical form, his *corpus.* He howled and the walls quivered and the puddle of light flickered. The Lurker tried to pluck the speck out, but that only added to the searing wrath and he fell to his knees. It was like a star blazing in his very core. He had met stars before, slain them, strewn their broken bodies across the cosmos as he gnawed upon their souls. He would *not* be beaten by this tiny bead of wrath stuck between his bones.

The Lurker looked up. *You.* The creature, the *human*, still pointed the primitive weapon at him, shaking, as the metal clicked and twitched and jerked in its hand. The Lurker roared, fueled by the rage, the energy of the burning star in his chest, then he leapt at the creature.

It screamed for a long time after that.

Rathford I

"Scissorhands?"

"It fits the M.O., don't it?"

Detective Charles Rathford had to admit that it did. The victim's wounds looked like someone had strapped foot-long razor blades to their fingers and gone ballistic.

"You sure we don't have footage from the security cameras?"

"I've told you three times. No. We got no security footage. The company uses an old system, and the tapes ran out at 11:42 p.m."

How did all of the tapes run out at the same time? Weren't those things supposed to last all night? And who used video tapes for security systems anymore? Rathford shook his head. Fucking bullshit.

Rathford held a handkerchief to his nose and knelt down to get a better look at the victim. He took a pen from his pocket and pulled back the drop cloth that covered the security officer.

Walton blanched and looked away. The man's chest cavity had been nearly vacated. The spine and—strangely enough—the heart were intact, but that was pretty much it. It was hard to tell which organ belonged to which corpse, or even which organ was which at times, but they thought they found a stomach in the rafters, lungs shredded and splattered willy-nilly over the nearby shelves. No livers, though. Like they were stolen. Or eaten.

Walton cleared his throat, eyes locked on his shoes. "There are five other bodies. Same wound pattern. None near as bad, though. He had a gun, too, a revolver. Empty."

"Did he hit the perp?"

"Can't tell. There's no way we're going to be able to tell whose blood is whose in this mess. DNA's going to be a fucking nightmare."

Rathford rolled his eyes and glared at the officer. "Did you find a blood trail leaving the building?"

Walton coughed. "No. No footprints, either."

A slow breath escaped Rathford's lips, and he looked around. The other bodies were in varying states of carnage. Walton was right, though. None of them showed signs of the thorough desecration that the security officer did.

Desecration. Rathford rolled the word around in his head for a moment. Why did that word feel so right? He'd never been religious. Grew up in a Catholic family, but didn't know if he even believed in God, nowadays.

And yet, he couldn't shake the weight of that word. Desecration.

Rathford stood up as a sudden inspiration struck him. "Does this place have catwalks, Walton?"

"They're a bit squishy."

"Doesn't matter. Are they clear?"

"I guess so. Forensics cleared out of here, what, two hours ago."

"Show me."

———

Rathford and the police captain looked down at the gruesome scene. The officer heaved several times, trying to keep his lunch down.

"Use your hat."

"Wha?"

"Your hat. I know you're squeamish, but if you puke on my crime scene, both of us are gonna hang for it."

Walton yanked his hat off and held it in front of his face and his generous stomach rippled, but nothing came up. Rathford was glad that he hadn't eaten before. Even so, the bodies splayed out in front of him on the main floor of the building threatened to make him retch. The bodies and the gore leered at him, taunting him, almost.

"Did forensics get pictures from this angle?"

Walton shook his head.

"Get 'em back here, then. I want the whole of the warehouse from up here. Panoramas, too."

Rathford half expected his partner to object, but Walton simply murmured an affirmative. Maybe he saw what Rathford did. From the ground, the gore seemed to be simply haphazard destruction. Now, the poor corpses leered up at him, and Rathford could see—something. Arms and legs at angles too precise, too consistent to be unintentional. What he thought were random blood smears connected the corpses in almost graceful sweeps. He could nearly see the pattern they made, the grand sculpture of blood and meat and bone, like looking at a masterpiece drenched in graffiti.

It whispered to the dark places in his mind.

Rathford shuddered and turned away, gripping the handrail. Couldn't look at it now. Forensics would come back and take the pictures. He could look at it then, on paper or a computer screen. When it was less real.

The two made their way out of the building, and Rathford leaned against the wall as soon as the door closed. The smell of death was still there. It lingered in his nostrils. He snorted and shook his head. It would pass. He always got stuck with the worst cases. He didn't know if that was a compliment or not.

Shouting snatched Rathford from his reverie. He grabbed his wits and dashed around the corner. Two police officers were struggling with a wiry, black-haired man on the warehouse loading dock. The man rammed one of the officers into the wall and tossed the other bodily off the dock, where he landed with a wet crunch and howled, bone peeking out of his arm like a new sapling. The man had one of the officer's firearms. Rathford dropped to one knee, yanked his own pistol from his underarm holster, and brought it to bear on the man.

"Freeze!" said Walton, to Rathford's left.

The man on the dock was surprisingly well dressed, Rathford noticed. Silk suit. Polished shoes. Black hair, grey at the temples. A grin too wide, too tight, too many teeth.

"Drop the weapon." The words left Rathford's mouth, but they sounded far away.

The man only grinned wider and giggled. The officer on the ground moaned.

"You won't stop him, you know."

"Won't stop who?" Rathford found his voice again. "Who did this?"

The madman giggled again. "He's come, and you won't stop him." Slowly, he raised the gun.

"Drop it!" Rathford tightened his grip on his pistol, trying desperately to keep his breath under control. "We will fire!"

"You won't stop him. He will usher in a new age of blood and glory." The barrel of the gun continued to rise.

"Drop the fucking gun!" Walton sounded far away.

"He will be our new God. He will usher in a new—"

Rathford squeezed the trigger, the slide of his 9mm ramming back and ejecting the brass corpse of the bullet. His ears rang as the madman stumbled back. Rathford's finger plucked the trigger each time his sights rested on the man's torso, gently, smoothly, as if he were plucking out some sweet melody on a beautiful instrument. More smoking brass bodies rang on the concrete. Ragged holes popped through the madman's suit as he stumbled and listed but remained upright. Finally, the slide of Rathford's gun locked open. The madman listed back, then forward, steadying himself, Cheshire grin still stretched across his face, blood dripping from it now. He raised the gun, pointing it at Rathford. His hand trembled, and Rathford thought that even if the madman somehow managed to fire, he would probably miss. Rathford could see down the barrel of the gun, could almost sense the bullet lurking there in the darkness, thirsting for his blood. His heart quivered coldly in his chest.

The pistol tumbled from the crazed man's hand and clattered onto the ground. He took one trembling step forward and coughed. Blood and spittle ran between his teeth and down his chin. He fell to his knees, then down onto the concrete.

Walton moved past Rathford, going to check the man's pulse, probably. A formality. Nobody could take that much lead and survive. Rathford simply lowered his pistol, trying to get control of his breathing. He quietly slipped out the spent magazine from his pistol and pulled out a new one. He was just sliding it in when a yelp made him drop it.

Rathford jerked his head up as Walton fell on his ass and scrambled backwards. He stared wide eyed at the man bleeding on the ground.

"What is it?" Rathford asked.

"He's looking at me."

"What the hell are you talking about?" Rathford grabbed his fallen mag and walked over to the corpse. "There's no way he can—" Rathford flinched. The dead man *was* looking at him. His eyes flickered between Rathford and Walton as blood seeped out of his nostrils and from between his teeth.

Rathford II

Rathford locked eyes with the dead man, the man that had no right to be moving—but was—and trembled. He took a step back, then another. The dead man's eyes flicked to Walton, then to Rathford. The grin widened.

"Fuck this." Walton's gun was in his hand, pointed at the dead man's face.

"Wait! Wait."

Walton looked at him.

"Call an ambulance," said Rathford.

"What? Are you out of your fucking mind?"

"Do it."

Rathford looked at the dead man, who lay in a pool of his own gore, then walked over to him and sank down, careful not to kneel in the blood. There was a lot of blood. Rathford pressed his finger to the man's neck, avoided looking at his eyes, but he could feel the dead man's gaze. The flesh beneath his fingers was warm but still. Rathford held his breath, pushed his fingers deeper into the flesh where the man's jaw met his neck, but there was nothing. The dead man's lips twitched. Rathford shook his head. No, they didn't. They couldn't have. The man was dead.

Rathford stood up, walked away, left a trail of bloody footprints. Walk. Don't run. The man was dead. The hairs on the back of his neck prickled, as if some great beast were behind him, waiting for him to turn around before it pounced. Rathford straightened his jacket.

There was no reason to be afraid of a dead man.

"He's got no pulse. He's dead. Call it in."

"Like hell he is. He's staring straight at you."

"He's dead, Walton. He isn't looking at anyone. It's just—" Rathford paused. "Muscle spasms."

A cough or a laugh came from behind him and Walton scrambled away, dragging his ass along the pavement.

"Muscle spasms," Rathford repeated.

Walton looked at him in disbelief, then back to the corpse on the ground. Slowly, he pushed himself to his feet, eyes never leaving the corpse. Even when he reached for the radio perched on his shoulder, his eyes remained locked on the body. The radio crackled, the sound of ripping fabric.

"This is Lieutenant Walton. We've had an officer-involved shooting."

"Roger, Walton. An ambulance is on the way. Were there any fatalities?"

Walton paused, looked at Rathford, at the corpse, then back to Rathford.

"Officer Walton, were there any fatalities?" The dispatcher sounded annoyed.

Walton licked his lips and turned away from Rathford and

the corpse. "The perp's got no pulse, but we've got two injured officers. One with a broken arm, one with a concussion."

"Roger. The ambulance is on the way."

Walton's hand fell from the radio at his shoulder as if the string that held it there had been cut. He shook his head. Rathford walked away. Just as he came to the corner of the warehouse, he heard Walton say something about the zombie apocalypse.

Rathford didn't look back.

The warehouse was a couple of miles outside the city. Lucky. Easier to control the spread of information. Rathford walked along the outside of the warehouse, gravel crunching under his heels. If people knew about a slaughter of this magnitude, they'd panic. Crunch, crunch, like bones grinding against each other. How many bodies had they found, again? Five? Six? The plink of breaking glass. He was glad he didn't have to handle the press, they'd have a—wait what?

Rathford looked down. Under his feet were dozens of shards of broken glass. Oh, fucking hell. He looked up to see the jagged teeth of a broken window and the mess of drying blood beyond. He almost vomited again. Worse, he'd contaminated his own crime scene.

Fucking idiot. He shook his head, looked around. There was nobody on this side of the warehouse. Trees on the other side of a chain-link fence that had a great tear in it. He looked down again. The forensics crew had probably already photographed this area. Probably. He found the edge of where the glass had fallen, and leapt, deer like, to where the gravel was free of glass, then turned back and sat down on his heels, looked over the damage. One, two footprints. He shook his head. If you didn't know what you were looking for, it was just more broken glass. He doubted anyone would ever notice.

Rathford took out his phone. He shot a picture of the scene as a whole, then zoomed in on each damning footprint. He'd never live this down. He looked up and photographed the window as well, what was left of it. Might as well. As he was putting his phone away, a thought occurred to him.

Why was the glass on the outside of the window?

He looked up at the other windows on this side of the building. They were all intact. He cocked his head and tried to remember if any of the other windows were broken as well. No, this was the only one. When he was looking over the scene the first time, he'd assumed that this window was how the perp had gotten into the building.

But if that were true, the glass would be broken inwards instead of outwards.

He looked back to the glass. The edges of some of the shards were off color, cloudy. He retrieved the pen from his chest pocket and gingerly lifted one of the shards with the tip. The substance was easy to miss, nearly clear, sticky. Strange. He let the shard fall back to the ground, pulled out his phone, photographed again, this shard specifically, then laid the phone on the ground without turning off the screen. He wrapped his fingers in his handkerchief, picked up the shard, brought it close to his face. It was dried ichor or spittle. He sniffed, jerked his head back. Acrid, harsh, like a laboratory. His nostrils tingled. He set the shard back where he'd plucked it from the ground, grabbed his phone and stood, and looked back to the building.

So this was where the perp exited the building. Any cameras? Lights? One, two lights. Soot coated the insides of one, and it glared at him like an empty eye socket. The other seemed intact. A camera on the corner, facing this direction.

Rathford made a mental note to check the footage later, then remembered what Walton had said to him again and again.

We ain't got no fucking footage.

His lips pursed and he looked back to the fence, strewn in pieces, almost as if a bear or a truck had barreled through it, but the gravel lacked the tracks of either. Even the top bar was in two pieces.

What the hell was going on here?

Rathford walked to the fence, watching the ground. Small divots, the size he would expect to see from a person. He looked at the fence. It was torn from top to bottom. No, torn was the wrong word. He knelt and inspected one of the severed links. Cut. The metal had been sheared, almost as if someone had taken a bolt cutter to the fence.

"Rathford!"

He started, pitched back onto his ass. It was Walton.

"Ambulance is here. They're loading the shooter. Just wanted you to know that they're creeped the fuck out, too. He's still looking at people."

Rathford rolled his eyes and pulled himself to his feet. "You've been watching too many zombie flicks, Walton. It's going to your head."

"Hey! I ain't the only one who's freaked out by that guy. The paramedics wouldn't even get close to him until I had my gun on him."

"Whatever." Rathford shook his head and motioned to the severed fence. "Has anyone gone this way?"

Walton shook his head. "We brought the K-9 unit in earlier. You know Bobby and Tank, right?"

Rathford nodded.

"Well, Bobby brought him over here, but Tank started

howling like someone was going after him with a club. He wouldn't stop until Bobby put him back in his car."

"Really? Bobby's always bragging about how Tank chased off a black bear on that one camping trip."

"Yeah, man. Something spooked him real bad."

Rathford sighed, looked back to the fence. "So nobody's been this way?"

Walton shook his head.

Rathford stooped, peered deeper into the forest, down a trail of mangled trees and shrubs. He jumped over what was left of the fence. Footprints. "I thought you said there were no tracks."

"Do those look like boot prints to you?"

Rathford crouched. No, he supposed they didn't, but he didn't say anything. They made him think of dog tracks, but he was no animal expert and they were entirely too large, regardless. Rathford took out his phone again, laid his pen next to the print for scale and took one, two, three photographs. Then he took photographs of the trail, then back at the building.

Walton still watched him.

"Call the forensics crew," said Rathford. "See if they took prints. If they didn't, I want 'em."

"What do you think they are?"

"You ever seen those shoes with the animal tracks on the bottom of the tread?"

"Yeah. My son wants a pair. Says he wants to scare a girl he knows. Elementary school crushes, right?" Walton gave a half laugh then swallowed.

Rathford nodded, waved at the prints, then retrieved his pen and stood. "Our little sicko thinks he's clever." He slipped the pen into his coat pocket. "It'll just make him easier to track down."

Walton didn't look too sure. He pushed his jaw sideways, cocked an eyebrow, looked at his shoes, then back at Rathford. "Wait, you're not thinking of following that trail, are you?"

Rathford shrugged. "Why not? Perp's almost certainly long gone by now. Besides, the longer we wait the more likely it is that some rabbit or something is going to run off with something important."

"I don't know, man." He trailed off. "I mean if Tank—" He ran a hand through his hair. "There's just something wrong with this whole fucking case."

"Too many zombie flicks, Walton."

"It ain't the fucking zombie flicks!" Walton's shout hung in the air, roused a murder of crows, who flew off cackling. Walton froze, looked at the sky. His shoulders were hunched and he stood on his toes like a cornered cat. Once the last of the crows' calls had faded, he looked back to Rathford. "Fine. Do what you want. Just don't get yourself killed out there."

Rathford rolled his eyes and patted his underarm holster. "I've got a gun and a phone. I think I'll be fine."

Walton threw his hands up and stormed off. Rathford smirked and shook his head, then turned to the footprints. They led into the woods, less a trail and more a vein of destruction. Branches and shrubs alike were torn asunder, cut, and broken. The trail was darker than it had any right to be, and it leered at him like a maw, as if he were a minnow and it the mouth of a great sea beast. He took a step back, pulse beating at his eardrum so hard it was as if his very blood were willing to void his body if only it did not have to go down that trail. He swallowed. Maybe Walton would come with him. Rathford turned, but Walton was already gone and Rathford was very much alone. He was about to call out, then stopped himself. With how much shit he'd just given Walton, he'd look the fool if he called for help now. He turned back to the woods and swallowed again and his pulse beat louder. *I'm making a big deal out of nothing*, he told himself. Nothing was down that trail, and the longer he waited the greater chance some vital clue would be lost. A coyote carrying off a bit of discarded clothing. A bit of torn cloth fluttering away in the wind. The overcast sky making good on the threat of rain.

He couldn't afford that, and he was just delaying now. It would be easier once he started. He took one step, then another, but his heart only beat harder, breathing came louder. What was wrong with him? There was nothing to be afraid of, nothing at all. He continued, deeper into the woods, following the trail of broken branches and unnatural footprints.

The forest seemed to get darker the deeper he went. Impossible, he told himself. These woods are not that thick. He'd been through them before. You could see the sky any time you looked up. He did so, but found that he could not. No blue or grey or hints of sunlight. Solely a bleak canopy of black, expansive and eternal, as if the sun itself had been swallowed up, as if the sky had never existed at all. He shuddered, looked back at the trail.

I should go back, he thought. He began to turn, but stopped. Walton would never let him live it down. Besides, his mind was just playing tricks on him. Rathford continued down the trail.

A twig snapped and Rathford jumped, hand going immediately to his pistol. He listened, peered into the forest. There was nothing. No sound or whisper of wind. No animal or insect calls. Graveyards were not this quiet. He looked down and found that it had been his own foot that had crushed the twig. He laughed. More of a giggle, high pitched and tinged with hysteria. His own damn foot. He laughed harder, louder, found he could not stop. He was shaking, but he could not stop that either. The trees leered at him, the severed branches and twigs like broken bones and gnarled fingers reaching out for him, eager to tear his skeleton from out his flesh and plant it among them.

Something touched his neck.

He whirled, pistol in hand, and fired. The shots echoed in the dead wood, then died themselves.

There was nothing.

He was panicking. He recognized the symptoms. He forced himself to lower his pistol when a sudden shock to his leg made him jump.

It was his phone. He pulled it out. Walton. Rathford answered it and put it to his ear.

"We heard gunshots. You okay?"

Rathford swallowed. "Yeah. Yeah." He looked around at the motionless wood. "It was just a deer. He spooked me."

The wood was silent. Walton sighed in his ear, said, "Maybe you should come on back. We can get a team of dogs in from—"

"I'm fine." Louder than he had intended. He swallowed. "I'm fine." Quieter this time. "It's just this crazy case. It's got everyone on edge."

Walton said nothing.

"I'll be fine. I'll keep my gun out, just in case."

A sigh. "Fine. You're the boss." A pause. "But I want it on record that I advised against this."

"Noted." Rathford's jitters were calming down; the phone no longer rattled against his ear. "I appreciate the concern. I'll buy you a beer this weekend."

"I'll hold you to that."

The line went dead.

Rathford drew in a deep breath, let it out through his nose. The trees seemed to loom less closely, but he still felt uneasy.

He looked back the way he came and was surprised at how far away it looked. Maybe he should do what Walton said, let the department borrow some dogs from the state.

No. He shook his head, rubbed his nose with the back of his hand. He pulled the magazine from his pistol, checked how many rounds he had expended. Three. Usually he was better about keeping track. He reinserted it and checked the woods again. Nothing.

He started to put his phone away but stopped as an idea struck him. He passed the phone to his off hand and began to record.

Rathford III

"This is Detective Charles Rathford. The date is the seventh of June. I am currently following the trail of a presumed suspect leading away from a crime scene." The glare from the phone seemed harsh against the bleak, dark woods, and he wondered if the contrast would keep his eyes from adjusting to the dark.

Rathford took a half step forward, hesitated, turned.

"I have come roughly—" The light that leaked in from the trailhead seemed small and far away. It showed up on his screen as little more than a white, overexposed blotch no bigger than a nickel, but even so it burned his eyes. He couldn't have come that far, could he? "—a dozen yards from the scene of the crime. The trail is at least eight hours old."

Back to the trail, which seemed darker than before. He blinked away the afterimage of the trailhead, but when it was gone the trail seemed no easier to see. Maybe he should turn on the flashlight; no, it was nine in the morning.

"I am currently alone. A K-9 unit attempted to follow the trail earlier, but experienced—" For some reason, the thought of Tank shunted into his brain, the brash German shepherd hemming and hawing, hiding behind Bobby's legs, braying, howling, digging his feet into the gravel as Bobby must have dragged him. He could almost hear the dog's anguished cries and found that they mirrored those of his own soul. "—difficulties."

Rathford angled the camera at the forest floor. It was barely visible on the screen, so he squatted, focused on one of the footprints. "I am currently following these tracks. They appear to be canine in nature, but they are most likely some sort of novelty shoe print."

He stood. Down the trail once more.

"The trail has been easy to follow so far. In fact, it almost seems like—" Like some ancient carnivore, full of rage and hate, had carved its way through the wood, tearing asunder everything that had stood in its way. "—like the suspect made this trail intentionally." Rathford forced his legs into motion.

The trail seemed to have no destination, leading this way and that, at times towards the highway as Rathford would have expected, at times deeper into the woods, cutting back upon itself, as if the one who had made it was either lost or had no thought on his mind other than the savaging of innocent shrubbery. Rathford made note of this aloud. Speaking seemed to help, or perhaps the act of recording itself. Either way, the darkness seemed held at bay; no less perhaps, but no longer encroaching upon him, seeping into his pores, into his gums, into his eyes. It might have been easier to navigate the dark woods without the fluorescent burn of the screen digging into his eyes, but Rathford found himself unwilling to turn the brightness down. As if it were his only light in this unholy place, as if he were a lone sojourner, lost upon the banks of the Styx.

Rathford nearly chuckled at that, but held it back for the sake of whomever might watch the video later. He would be in a sorry state indeed if he had nothing but a phone to light his way in the underworld.

Maybe the boatman would take his phone instead of a coin under the tongue.

He wondered what time it was, but not aloud. The trail seemed endless, meandering, almost hypnotic. It left him dizzy, sluggish, but that was probably due to the fact that he had not yet broken his fast. An old habit of his, but one that often left him drained by midmorning. It must be around 10 o'clock by then. A new panic encroached then, that of his battery, his location. He must have been following this trail for an hour or more, and he was no longer sure that he could find his way out again, or how much longer before his phone was quenched by the dark. He contemplated opening a map, or at least tabbing away from the camera so that he could check the time, the battery. Surely the phone would keep recording even if the program was running in the background, wouldn't it? Even if it didn't, a few moments gone undocumented couldn't hurt, right? Yet, he recorded on.

He couldn't even check his watch; he had gotten out of the habit of wearing one years ago. They felt like weighty beetles on his wrist, skittering back and forth, pinching out his hairs.

Perhaps he should invest in a pocket watch.

Regardless, it was only a matter of time before—and there it was. A message informed him that his phone had twenty percent battery remaining and asked if he would like to go into low-power mode. He decided against it, dismissed the pop-up, then second-guessed his decision. It wouldn't have changed anything, would it? Almost certainly not. Why hadn't he opted for low-power mode? Now he would have to tab away from the

camera function to activate it, which he could not bring himself
to do. He swallowed. It wasn't the end of the world. The phone
would notify him when it reached ten percent, and he would
have the chance to extend his battery life then.

A sudden blinking caught his eye, the timer that kept track
of how long he had been recording. Of course, how could he
have—he blinked, rubbed his eyes and blinked again. That
couldn't be right. The numbers that should have indicated how
long he had been recording were flashing.

00:66:66

00:66:66

00:66:66

He laughed, high-pitched and eerie. Then he forced a
cough. Had to hold it together. You never know who might
watch this later.

It must just be a bug. He didn't know much about program-
ming, but he knew that it could fuck up in strange and unpre-
dictable ways, especially when the program encountered things
the developers might not have planned for. That's it. It must just
be the low-power pop-up screwing with the camera timer.

Nothing more.

He pulled his eyes away from the screen to the trail of
wreckage that he followed, heart pounding in his ears, at his
throat, at his wrists. Keep moving forward. His voice cracked
now, and he found that he was speaking less. He should be
speaking *more*. Make the most of these last few minutes before
—before what? Nothing would happen when the phone ran
out of battery. He would simply be out a useful tool to docu-
ment what happened. Nothing more.

"Nothing more."

The screen flashed again. It was another box telling him
that he was down to ten percent. How could that be? He had

barely come a dozen steps, hadn't he? He looked behind him, but found no useful reference point, simply broken branches and uprooted brush.

Back to the screen. He had a decision to make now. Keep recording? Or try to preserve what remained of his power in case he needed it later? Behind the dialogue box the time readout blinked: 00:66:66.

He took a deep breath before putting the phone into low-power mode and closing the camera. With how his phone was behaving, he probably only had another thirty seconds of video, anyway. What to do with the nine percent that remained? His eyes flashed to the woods around him, then returned to the screen.

Walton. He checked how many bars he had. One, just one, but he was on a data network, thank God.

He attached the video to a text and sent it to Walton. Did large file transfers still go through even if you went to another program? Or were they like that cat Schrödinger had murdered, and you had to watch them or it didn't happen? Rathford didn't know, so he watched the progress bar crawl across the screen as his battery ticked down to seven percent, six percent.

An error message popped up: *File Too Large*.

Rathford nearly pitched his phone into the dark.

Rathford IV

Calm. Must be calm. It didn't matter, anyway. Now that he thought about it, there was no real reason to send the file to Walton. There would be time for Rathford to review it once he got back to the precinct. He clicked the phone closed, and the darkness enfolded him completely, but he clenched his teeth and let out a long, slow breath. Just the dark. Nothing more. His thumb flicked the switch to take the phone off vibrate. No, that was a bad idea. What would happen if he stumbled on the perp and his phone went off? He flicked it back to vibrate and the phone shuddered in his palm. Shit, the battery. He clicked the screen on.

Five percent.

To hell with it. Rathford shook his head, stuffed the phone in his pocket, but this time the dark closed in on him like a wave of sap—sticky, viscous, warm. He couldn't breathe, as if the tenacious shadows had replaced the very air with their essence, and he felt like a moth which had landed in as-yet uncrystallized amber.

He tried to breathe, but his lungs seized, as if themselves terrified of the encroaching, eternal dark. As if the that deep bleakness were a terrible solvent, a celestial turpentine come to dissolve him whole, leaving nothing but a memory of his passing, a whisper of a being once called Rathford. In the end his need for fresh air won and he inhaled, and he knew his lungs had been right to refuse the darkness entrance, for it sank into his gums, blank tendrils of oblivion, pushing and worming betwixt his teeth as if to push them out every one and replace them like dark saplings. It slid down his throat like black pitch and squirmed in his bosom, elemental and primal. It wormed into his ears, into his eye sockets, tickling his nerves like oiled feathers as it made its way to his brain. He tried to scream, but only a strangled wheeze escaped his lips. Another breath, another lungful of oblivion, and he screamed again, a bat-like wail.

His hand immediately went to his pocket. Fuck the battery, he needed light, needed it like his ancestors who had once crouched before their fires, their wards against the dark. He delved into his pocket only for his hand to be caught in a snarl of twisted fabric. He pushed, tugged, but his fingers found no purchase and came no closer to that tiny electric flame that would ward off the dark, if only for a few moments more. A whimper escaped his throat and he pushed harder, heedless of the sound of tearing fabric. He could feel it there, bouncing against his leg, silhouetted by tangled cloth as the dark pulled him ever closer like the grasp of an unwanted lover.

Run! He had to run. He lurched into motion, heedless of obstacles. Branches reached out to seize him, tore at his face, at his clothes, at his soul. Roots, or maybe the great tentacles of unnameable beasts, tripped him up, sending him sprawling. Screams hounded him, the howls of exiled beings, cast out when the foundations of the world were laid, banished with the light of the new sun. He could not escape; he knew this with the certainty that any deer or rabbit or fly knows that its time has come, and like that prey he ran on, bereft of hope and full of nameless terror.

He tripped, and he knew this time it would be the end of him. He would never rise again, and his bones would never be found. Before he hit the ground he contemplated briefly the beer that he owed Walton, wondered how long it would be before they started searching for him. The impact stole from him what little breath he had, and he curled upon himself like a pill bug, knees against his chest and arms about his head, trembling and wheezing. He knew not how long he laid there, body tense against the coming talons and teeth, but none came.

He opened his eyes.

A subtle glow suffused the clearing. He sat up, looked about him. It was like pale moonlight, bleak and harsh and cold and small. Shadows fled from the bases of the bonelike and gnarled trees, but did not flee far, meeting the great writhing dark mere paces from the edge of the clearing. He looked about to find the origin of that pale glare and gasped.

In the center of the clearing stood a great beast. A cervid, but greater, taller than any deer or elk or even moose, a paragon of that family, as if the father of all things that wore antlers about their heads. He was taller than Rathford at the shoulder, and had six legs, seven eyes, four ears, and a crown of antlers that had no end of branches and points, but seemed to become part of the canopy itself, as if it held in those horns a connection to all the woods of the world. Nestled among those endless branches, he seemed to hold the very moon captive, harsh and uncaring and cruel. The great beast glared at him as he lay sprawled upon the forest floor, eyes aglow with the same light as the captive moon. Rathford could not hold those eyes for long, for he found his soul pierced with shame, as if the light laid bare all his flaws and sins before this great animal who stood in silent witness to his imperfections. When he looked up at the beast again, he found that it had looked away and he felt some relief, for he did not think he could bear the creature's eyes a second time. Rathford followed the creature's gaze and saw something he thought he might never see again.

Daylight. An archway of piercing light no bigger than his outstretched hand.

When Rathford glanced back to the cervid it had turned, striding deeper into the woods, the cold light it carried with it already receding until Rathford found himself at the twilight between the uncaring moon and the hungry dark. He turned to the hole of daylight in that dark firmament, and it seemed to be smaller, farther away. He was not sure he could reach it before the quivering dark seized him again. A lump formed in his throat and he gulped, scrambling to his feet, and he turned to follow the creature that bore the moon in his crown. No sooner than he had taken a step than the great creature spun and reared, bellowing a challenge that made Rathford tremble. It lowered its head in challenge and pawed the ground, and Rathford scrambled backwards, deciding that perhaps whatever lurked in the dark would be better than being impaled on this creature's horns.

He turned and was hesitating at the line between the light and dark when another bellow chased him into motion. A glance back and he found that the creature, whatever it was, had disappeared entirely. He fixed his eyes on the bright piece of daylight and ran as hard as he could. No more than a hundred yards. He could make it. The howls of the damned chased him. Eighty yards. Something snagged his suit coat but he tore himself free, abandoning it like an anchor. Fifty yards. Black tendrils, or perhaps just roots snaked around his feet and ankles, but Rathford kept his footing. Twenty five yards. Bony fingers or—more likely—spiny twigs whipped at his flesh, tore at his clothes. Finally, Rathford burst forth from the woods, slowing falling to his knees in a wide field of foxtail. A house sat not far away, and beyond that a quiet rural road well paved but free of cars.

Rathford's ragged breath and a gentle breeze were the only sounds that broke the peace. His throat burned and he swallowed, reaching up to loosen his tie. He shook his head and ran a hand through his hair. What the fuck had just happened?

He looked over his shoulder at the dark wood and shuddered, turning away in as much shame as fear. A few minutes alone in a dark wood and he had completely lost it, his mind conjuring up monsters. A seven-eyed deer-creature? He considered scheduling an appointment with the precinct shrink. He'd almost certainly lose his job. And they'd be right to sack him. He had some vacation time he could use. Once this case was cracked, he could take a lengthy leave of absence and let these demons shake themselves out of his head. He should go back and get his coat. It had been expensive. But when he turned back to the forest, that solemn archway leered at him, shadows nearly spilling out into the field, and his heart seized in his chest and refused to beat any more until he turned away.

On second thought, he had other suits.

He stood, brushing off his knees, plucking the foxtail from his trousers, straightening and cinching his tie, then trying to part his hair to one side with his fingers. It wouldn't do to look like some crazed schmuck when he got to the house and asked to use their phone.

Lurker II

Rage. Rage like the Lurker had never felt before, buried deep in his chest, caking around the tiny bit of metal that *insipid* human's weapon had lodged inside him, that impossibly small star that burned in his core. He howled, the enclosure shuddering and the tiny eyelike suns sputtering in their sockets. His claws twitched, needed to be buried in soft human flesh once again, but the scattered corpses about him did not move or bleed any longer. Not even the last one, the fat one, the insolent creature who had lodged this thrashing quasar in his bosom.

Away. It was hard to think with this blaze nestled in his chest. *I must be away from this place.* He ran to one of the rectangular holes in the walls and jumped through, shattering the crystalline pane which separated him from the outside. He landed in a small field of broken pebbles and one of the miniature suns set at the top of the building flashed and died. Another flickered as the Lurker passed.

A legion of beings stood before him, unmoving. They were

tall, two, three, four times the Lurker's own height, with many fractal arms that branched into many fingers, holding up a great crown. The Lurker nearly laughed. He knew the humans could not be the greatest creatures on this sphere, but he had not expected to be found quite so quickly. No matter. These old souls would be more enjoyable to rend and swallow than the humans had been.

He charged, nearly forgetting the sun thrashing in his chest, and tore through the net of metal that stood between him and his foes, then he was among them ripping into their stiff and matted flesh. He had already severed a dozen limbs when he realized that they made no move to stop him or strike at him, or even any move at all.

The Lurker stopped and spun around, confused. Had he miscalculated? Did these creatures not have souls far older than the humans'? Why did they not move, not strike out? He tore another limb from a nearby creature; he felt its fear and dismay, but it did nothing. He lashed out again and again, but the creatures did nothing.

The Lurker howled. He had expected *violence. Mayhem. Destruction.* Something to occupy the rage that boiled in his chest and in his soul. He tore into creature after creature, hewing limbs and flesh, but the creatures did nothing for their own defense, and the star in his chest lashed him with every stroke. He ran and struck out at the life around him, tearing, ripping, clawing, biting, visiting the searing, jittering anger in his chest on the life that surrounded him.

But it was not enough. No matter how many of these ageless pillars he flayed it was never enough. Their clear, sticky blood clung to his claws. He could strike all of them down, leave this place a wasteland, but it would make the searing no less.

Humans. I will visit this insolence of their kind on them a thou-

sandfold. Until the stars all die and the cosmos folds in upon itself. I will make myself their God and they will worship me as I gnaw upon them.

The Lurker ran, lashing and tearing as he went. He had to find more humans. More prey to quiet this squirming star in his bosom.

He burst forth from the petrified beings that canopied him off from the sky into a vast field of skinny, brittle filaments that reached past his knees, each burdened with tiny spined wombs at their tips. Tiny souls, each one, like wisps of dust cast upon stellar winds, but there were so many of them. This world's star was crawling over the horizon, and the Lurker skidded to a halt, covering his eyes and blinking until the sparks in his eyes died. The Lurker had always been opposed to light, and it to him, but with this lanky encapsulation of flesh and bone, it seemed somehow worse, his flesh crawling, prickling, burning. Black smoke curled from his skin wherever the light touched him. The rays made his skin crawl and bunch, made his hairs stand on end, made the star in his chest thrash harder, as if in sympathy to the greater one set in the sky. The Lurker spread his claws and roared at it as it rolled over the horizon, as if to claim this sphere in its entirety for himself. The howl echoed and all else fell silent. For a moment, it seemed that the sky darkened and the sun shrank back on the horizon.

The moment passed and the sun continued his course. The Lurker snorted. He could endure the steaming, prickling light for a while longer; there would be plenty of time to take care of *him* later. Later, when he had shed this prison of bone and sinew. Nebulas of grey and black distilled on the horizon and began to spread across the sky, and the Lurker growled to himself as he scanned the expanse. Empty, save for a long black scar that cut it in half and disappeared into the columns of ageless flesh, and a curious rectangular thing that protruded from the earth. It had a peaked crown and was colored red and white. Curious, but unremarkable. The Lurker nearly turned away from it when he noticed the portals in the walls of the thing, not unlike the crystalline portal of the place where he had first arrived on this world. His hair electrified, stood on end, and the throbbing in his chest grew distant. There had been humans where he had first arrived.

Perhaps there would be humans here.

He ran, leapt, then crashed through the portal. A screech greeted him and the Lurker exulted. There it was, covering its face and howling, a mess of goop on the ground. It turned to run, but the Lurker leapt upon it, digging his claws into its soft flesh. It screamed, and static tingled through the Lurker's arms and back, quieting the star in his chest. No need for the precision he'd employed with the others. No, this one he could desecrate however he pleased. He was about to set his teeth into the thing when a small voice came from around the corner.

"Mommy? Mommy, what's—"

The sound stopped and the Lurker turned. A small creature stood in the entryway of an abutting chamber, an effigy of some strange fuzzy thing at its feet. Probably human. It had two legs and two arms and a—

It screamed. Unpleasant.

The Lurker snarled and tilted his head, then leapt at the tiny thing. It fell on its back and the Lurker sailed over it, rending great furrows across the ground as he skidded. The tiny human regained its feet and fled into another chamber with surprising quickness. The Lurker made to follow when a great black thing slammed into one of the chamber walls near the Lurker's head, then clattered to the ground. The first human, holding its side with one arm and an iron concavity in the other. "S-stay away from my child you— you—"

The insolent little— the Lurker flexed his claws, growled, stalked closer to the pitiful—wait. Was the human trying to—it was, wasn't it? He looked down the corridor where the tiny one had gone, and he laughed.

Delicious.

The Lurker leapt, leaving great gouges in the ground, ran along the walls of the corridor, bouncing from one to another, knocking the things that hung there to the ground. A great howl came from the human he had just left, and a giddy energy trembled across the Lurker's skin. He reached the end of the corridor, where there were three abutting chambers. Which one had the tiny thing gone into? He lifted his nose and sniffed. Not there. The larger human came around the corner and flung the dish at him. He batted it out of the air, sniffed again. Not there. Blood dripped from the big one as it came down the corridor at him, water dripping from its eyes and making curious sounds. Delightful sounds. But where—? There. The Lurker darted through the portal into the chamber and now he could hear tiny whimpers, tiny cries. They filled his bones with eagerness, and the engine in his chest beat faster, the quasar thrashed harder. The one was exhilarating, the other frustrating, distracting. But where was the tiny thing? He closed his eyes. A scream from the corridor. Sniff. Sniff. There—yes —there.

A growl budded in his chest and he opened his eyes, spun, and there was a new creature before him, something made of bone and fur and darkness, a crown of shadows on its brow. The Lurker started. He knew not where this one had come from, but he would rend him and gnaw on his soul as well. The Lurker leapt at his foe, and the other leapt to meet him in the air. Just as the Lurker was about to sink his teeth into his prey he struck something solid and brittle, and then the other fractured and flew apart and the Lurker struck the chamber wall, and slid to the ground in a snarl of fur and limbs. What—? Where had—? He regained his feet, and looked around, crunching and clinking beneath his feet. He danced away, spun around. Had he fled the plane? Folded away? He growled and the fur across his back stood on end.

"Come on. Come on, baby."

The humans. The big one had the little one in its arms and was limping down the corridor, leaving footprints of blood. The Lurker made to go after them, but glanced around the chamber once more. A large cushion in the middle of the room. Scattered shards on the ground. No sign of his foe. The Lurker growled. He might be waiting to pounce as soon as the Lurker turned his back. He spun around again, the muscles in his arms twitching and his claws full of need. Another whimper from the corridor, and the pair of humans disappeared around a corner.

No. These insolent things would not escape. Let the other one ambush him where it could; it was of no consequence. He dashed down the corridor. There they were. He scrabbled across the ground, trying to find purchase on the slickness. The big one looked back at the sound and screamed and then the little one screamed as well. Finally his claws found purchase, tearing out great gouges from the floor, and the Lurker pounced. The big one turned, shielding the tiny one with its body, and the Lurker's claws sank into its flesh as he knocked them to the floor. Eagerness filled his breath and he bit, reveling in its screams and struggles, until something struck him across the face.

The Lurker recoiled, then nearly laughed. The tiny one! It was holding that iron dish that had been flung at him! And now again it struck at him! He caught the primitive weapon, then grabbed the thing around the chest and pressed it to the ground, leaving the other bleeding and squirming. He pressed his weight down upon it, curious what it would do. It railed at him with tiny fists, chest spasming as its breath was crushed out of it. How long would it take before it stopped moving? The big one screamed, pulled at one of his legs, and the Lurker looked back. Its teeth were gritted and water was running from its eyes even as the life leaked out of its wounds. And yet, it still tried to protect this little one. How quaint. How lovely. He turned his body so that he was no longer between the big one and the small one, and watched as it tried to crawl towards him, the blood pooling around them. As it got closer, the Lurker lowered his head and held the little one's head in his jaws as it beat on his face.

"No! Please, no! No, no, no—"

The Lurker had no idea what the sounds it was making actually meant, but he had been around for long enough that he understood the idea behind them.

It was begging.

A shiver ran down the Lurker's back, through his hair and he found that he liked the feeling. Perhaps having a body wasn't so bad after all.

He snapped his jaws shut and the little one's skull shattered, the taste of blood and bone filling his mouth. Another shiver ran up his spine, a warm rush that made his flesh roil, one that quieted the burning in his chest.

The big one screamed.

No, not bad at all.

Lurker III

The Lurker sniffed. The tingle in his throat and the pleasant static running down his back were fading, and now the places where these primitives had struck him had started to pulse, to grind against his consciousness. The muscles in his jaw tensed and ground his teeth together, as if in protest to the strange sensations dancing along his nerves. He filled his lungs until his chest felt ready to burst, then blew it out again. There. Some relief. How quaint.

Nothing else stirred in this place. Nearly nothing. Smoke rose from a black slate, the slime upon it slowly blackening. Black specks buzzed near the crystal barrier that he had shattered, but none entered. He could taste their fear and laughed. The tiny things were cosmically beneath his notice, barely alive at all.

Then again, so were the humans, were they not? And yet they were such *fun* to murder.

The Lurker snorted. These two were dead, their blood cooling, soaking into the furred ground, souls evacuated. A pity. He was hungry, but he had been too distracted by the—*needs*—of the flesh to snatch their souls before they had evanesced. He huffed, irritated. A stupid mistake, one he had not made in a very long time. And yet, how overwhelming it had been, tearing into the soft, struggling bodies, the sweet screams, the blood speckling his face, his arms, his claws, like sparks igniting something inside this thing that he inhabited. This body, this bizarre—*corpus*. Something that had washed away his waking mind and replaced it with energy and need and heat. That need —his body trembled at the memory of it, and he felt it again, a shallow echo of it. It was like something had possessed him, and yet that thing was almost a more distilled, more pure version of himself.

But how could he be more himself, yet so divorced from control? The thought disturbed and excited him. He wanted more of it. Even time seemed suspended as he tore flesh and shattered bone, the screams and frothing blood splitting the air in an eternal singularity, all encompassing, all consuming. Nothing existed but his claws and his need and the human creature's flesh and its agony, and then all at once the thing lay unmoving before him, a steaming, hollow ruin, twitching at the memory of life.

He turned to the portal by which he had entered, but something held him. Something in his core, a quiet gnawing. Not the ridiculous, burning fraction of a star that was lodged in his chest, no. This was different. Lower. A grinding void, twisting flesh, a vortex that needed—something. And for some reason spittle distilled on his tongue and dribbled out his mouth in tiny rivulets. Some ran down his throat and his body swallowed, but that only seemed to make the gnawing void pull harder, as if it meant to pull him into himself and cannibalize his body.

Why were these bodies so burdensome?

He sniffed again and the fragrance that steamed from the two cooling humans sent a shudder down his spine. The unmoving mounds of flesh drew him in, as if he were some unsuspecting comet and they a star, and he bent, his chest thudding and his abdomen churning and groaning. He soon found himself with his nose nearly buried in the quivering flesh of the larger creature. Drool dribbled from his chin, his breath nearly steaming. He needed something from this human, needed it like he had needed to claw it apart, to hear its pain manifest, but what was it? There was nothing but warm meat. Listless matter slowly coming to equilibrium with the drifting air. And yet, he could not pull away. His jaws opened, as if on their own accord. This was absurd. He was a ravager of stars, a terror in the black, slayer of gods, hewer of— his tongue brushed the dripping flesh and the Lurker trembled. He swallowed, then ran his tongue along the meat. *This* is what he needed. His teeth sank into the flesh and he tore a chunk away, blood coating his tongue, running down his throat. He scarfed down the meat, a hunk so large it nearly caught in his throat as it slid down to the gnawing void in his abdomen. His body shook, electrified, skin bunching as warm, pleasant tingles danced from the base of his skull all down his back and across his shoulders, but the void inside him only churned more fiercely. He tore away more, scarfing it down as quickly as his breath would allow.

He had peeled nearly all the flesh from the larger human before the need abated, and the gnawing void inside him filled to an uncomfortable pressure. He looked down at himself and found that his abdomen had swollen. Quaint. Uncomfortable. Pleasant. Confusing. What had he done? Why did it fill him with these conflicting sensations? The Lurker licked his lips and stretched his limbs. He should be going. He had wasted too much time here already. Time. Time. How does one waste something that doesn't exist? He dropped to all fours and took a ponderous step towards the shattered crystal barrier, little shards plinking under his feet and claws. He grasped the opening with his claws, meaning to leap out, to start the hunt anew, but his muscles would not obey. They felt heavy, weak.

I must go. Time is against me.
There is time still. Stay. Rest.
But the Well of Souls...

The Well is going nowhere, and you will find nothing beyond light and tiny, impudent souls. Rest. .

The Lurker grumbled. It had been eventful since he'd arrived, hadn't it? Many new things to deal with. Sensations. Humans. Perhaps it was time to rest. Yes. The weight of this world seemed to drag down his eyelids, his hands.

He looked around the human dwelling. It was a cuboid enclosure, with a propensity of horizontal surfaces, all about the height of his hips. Some on stilts, some simply themselves large boxes, some suspended from the walls. Quaint. The human mind seemed to have an affinity for lines and angles. Unnatural. Strange.

But on one of the far sides of the enclosure, there was a pleasing puddle of darkness. The Lurker strode over to get a better look at it. A slope, depending below the proper level of the ground, studded with angular protrusions. At the bottom, darkness. Lovely, welcoming darkness.

The Lurker descended.

Rathford V

Rathford started across the field to the house. It would take him forever to get all the foxtail out of his slacks, but there was no help for it.

Goddamn weeds.

What time was it? Noon? That's what it felt like. He looked up. The sky was laden with clouds, growing darker. But no rain. Rathford patted his pocket for his phone, then slipped a hand inside. The cloth was twisted in a parody of a whirlpool, and the place where the pocket and his slacks overlapped there were several holes. The memory of his panic and the tearing fabric seeped back, and he pushed it away, face burning. Twelve years on the force, five of them as a detective, and he'd panicked like a little girl waking up from a nightmare. A question tickled the back of his mind, however.

How in God's name had his pocket gotten snarled so quickly? It had only been, what, a second, maybe two, after he'd dropped his phone in there in the first place, right? He untwisted his pocket and extracted the thing, clicked it on. The screen flashed white, then black. Rathford cursed, slid it back into his pocket.

It didn't matter. He was nearly at the house now, and he'd be able to ask—to ask—

One of the windows was broken in.

Blood from that morning welled behind his eyes, as if newly shed. The stench of it, nearly an inch deep in some places, set up like pudding, sticking to his shoes. The smell of guts and shit and—

His hand drifted to his gun. He shook his head. Stop. It was just a broken window. A broken window, by itself, meant nothing. Just some dorky kid with a baseball and a bat.

He quickened his step, ignoring the way the air dragged needles down the back of his throat, the way that his nostrils felt they were about to crack like a dead riverbed. His feet felt as if they were full of lead, clubbing the ground. He ran faster. Only fifty yards from the house now, and there was no movement, no sound beyond the foxtail whispering to him as he crushed it underfoot. His heart felt like a whale's in his chest; too large, too slow, thundering against his lungs, against his ribs, with each beat. His throat, dry, sticky, trapping all the oxygen in his larynx before it ever made it to his lungs, before it ever seeped into his blood.

He hadn't run like this since he was a beat cop.

His eyes darted all around the field. Something was

watching him, he could feel it on the back of his neck. Any sign? Any movement? Not in the house. Not in the foxtail. Not behind him, in that dark maw of the forest. On the ground ahead of him there were footprints. The same ones that he'd followed into the woods, now mixed with gashes in the soil.

He drew his pistol from his underarm holster.

Rathford reached the house at a dead run, and when he reached it he turned and let his momentum slam his shoulder against the siding. The brittle vinyl snapped, jabbed against his skin like broken LEGOs. He held his pistol near his face, and he smelled the burnt powder from earlier.

It smelled like death.

He peeked around the window frame into the house. One eye only, in the very corner of the window. He guessed he might look like some perverted owl to anyone who might see him. The broken glass jilted his vision: here were two faucets, offset, one larger than the other. The bow of a chair unconnected to a base. A light switch on the far wall, cut in half and sliding apart. He ducked away and slid under the window like a burglar then glanced through the other corner of the window with the other eye. Pancake batter going hard in a clear mixing bowl, blackened remnants upturned and smoking on a griddle. The smell of blood going cold, going to pudding, and then to a powdery mass the consistency of women's makeup as it cracked and peeled...

No. There's no smell of blood. You're panicking. You're having flashbacks from this morning. There is no blood.

Oh, but there is. There is, and you can smell it, you can taste it, feel it seeping out from under your fingernails. It is the very scent of fear. The first fear. The fear that screams down the aeons of time from the roar of the first predator and the shriek of the first prey.

You can't wait to taste it, can you?

Rathford swallowed, and slid down the siding like a raindrop, his shirt catching and the tails coming out of his slacks. His heart beat in his throat, cutting away his breath. He swallowed again, pushing it back down where it belonged, back into his chest before it could leap out of his mouth and flop on the ground like some misshapen fish.

The grips of his pistol dug into his hands, the little diamond crosshatch imprinting itself into his palms like a million little pins. He took a deep breath, closed his eyes and held the air in his chest. Out slowly through the nose and he opened his eyes again. He pushed himself into a crouch and slunk around the front of the house to the front door. He hammered on the door. "Police! Open up!" He waited half a dozen heartbeats, hammered again. No sound but the murmuring foxtail. He put his shoulder to the doorjamb and his hand on the doorknob and slowly began to turn it. The latch disengaged; he felt it, heard it, but when he pushed against the door with his shoulder it merely thumped and did not move. Deadbolt.

He stood back, looked left, right. There was a car in the gravel, half-circle driveway. A lawnmower on its side, blade, bolts, and tools in an arc between him and it. Half mowed, half yellowed grass. Foxtail. Murmuring foxtail. Not another house in sight.

He pulled his foot up to heel in the door, but stopped and put it down again. Was he really doing this? He stood for a moment in contemplation. One moment, two.

Yes. Yes, he was doing this. There was something *wrong* here. Something that lurked beneath the surface like a crocodile.

And if there wasn't he would pay for the fucking door himself.

Rathford sucked air and drove the heel into the door above

the knob. The door snapped open and rebounded against the wall and nearly slammed shut again, the brass tooth of the deadbolt slamming against the splintered trim. He shouldered it open. "Police! Nobody—"

Two bodies. Carpet, caked brown with blood long dried. Fragments of bone. Spatter. Giblets, scattered on the floor, on the walls, on the ceiling. The smell of it. Oh, God, the smell.

Rathford fell to his knees.

———

"You okay, boss?"

Rathford looked up, took the cup from Walton's hands, held it in his own. His fingers were cold, but the warmth of the coffee was slow to seep through the polystyrene.

"Yeah. I'm fine." He shifted where he sat on the rear end of the ambulance. "You wanna go over it again?"

"Nah. We got your statement. Besides, you got an alibi, right?" Walton's chuckle died before it got very far.

"Yeah. I suppose I do." The video on his phone. The coffee was hot, searing the tip of his tongue. Bitter. He preferred it cold, on the sweeter side.

Walton leaned on the corner of the ambulance next to him, drinking his own coffee. "Crazy shit, man."

"Yeah."

They watched the paramedics wheel out the bodies, one large and one small, a mother and her child, each clothed in black plastic, as if they were something shameful. Ambulance and police lights danced against the vinyl siding, too bright under the gloomy clouds. The smell— Rathford took another drink.

"You got anything stronger?"

"No, man. You know I don't do that no more."

A grunt. Another swig, draining the cup. "Too bad." He stood, handed the cup back to Walton. "Tell Jack I'm taking the rest of the day off."

"Yeah, man. Yeah. No problem. You need a ride? I mean, your car's back at the other scene."

Car. Hm. It was, wasn't it? The thought hadn't occurred to him. As if cars had been entirely erased from his mind. Black paint. Faux leather. Needles. Dials. Speakers. These were what made up a car, right? Pedals, too, he guessed. The lurch of acceleration and the blur of a world whizzing by.

He'd honestly been about to just start walking.

Rathford VI

Rathford hauled himself to his feet. There was a draining feeling in his temples and face, and sight, hearing, direction trickled away. As if the world had ceased to be. No sound, no light, no matter or substance. Only Rathford and his weakening body that seemed to be another entity entirely. He knew at that moment that if he fell, he would fall forever. He would fall between the lines, like he had so many times in life, forgotten, overlooked, middle child.

But this time it would be different. This time he would fall and pass into nothingness to fall for all eternity. Forgotten. A whisper. A wraith with his face pressed against the glass as the rest of the world went about its business and he watched on, forever excluded.

Then there was the world again. A gravel driveway. Emergency vehicles. Officers. Yellow tape. The busted door and the dripping scene beyond, blood blackening and the room buzzing with flies and forensics workers. He wondered if he would get this scene, too, if they were connected. They almost certainly were. A psychopath with wolf boots going on a killing spree.

The scene came before his eyes again, almost physical. The woman and her child, blood-soaked carpet, walls covered in spatter and giblets and—Rathford shook his head, bringing his hand up over his face, rubbing his temples. No animal on earth could tear someone apart like that. A bit of bile rose in his throat and he swallowed, not wanting to lose his coffee.

"You comin'?"

"Yeah. Yeah." Rathford let his hand slide down his face, tugging his cheeks down and pulling his eyes open. As if he might see further, see better. See what and where and why. Most of all, why. Why would anyone—?

But that was for another time. Back at his desk, back where he could think, look at all the little pieces in isolation, find the connections, the lines among the evidence that would trap the killer in a web of his own making. Where he wasn't so close to what had happened. Not that it should be hard. This looked like a rampage more than a carefully executed series of murders. Victims of opportunity rather than of selection.

But that was for later, back at his desk, where the stench of it didn't hang in the air. His mouth wet and his stomach constricted and he knew if he didn't leave soon, he would leave with an empty stomach.

He walked toward Walton's vehicle, but before he had covered half the distance, the sky trembled and grew dark, a wave of thunder rolling through his bones. As if lightning had struck without a flash. Or, rather, the opposite of a flash. As if a piece of the void had smeared down through the atmosphere and struck the earth.

The crime scene stopped moving, went silent. Everyone

looked at the sky, their shoulders hunched, muscles tense, like rabbits upon hearing a twig snap. Breathless, ready to run until their hearts burst.

Then Rathford felt it. A presence crawling up his spine with spider legs. His eyes gravitated towards the shattered door, and he found that where he had seen Dave and Steve taking their pictures, collecting evidence, he could no longer. Darkness lurked there like a physical thing, cloying, sticky, almost liquid. The mere sight of it made his thoughts tighten to the point that his breath came in gasps. It was like the darkness that had possessed the woods, a nearly tangible miasma.

"Dark in there, isn't it?"

"Yeah." Walton's voice sounded harrowed, as if he himself were barely able to keep himself from running.

They stood there for a long moment. Two. Three. Finally Rathford swallowed, shook his head. "Crazy case." He turned, strode towards Walton's car.

Walton stayed for a moment longer. Rathford opened the passenger side door, looked back to his friend. "You coming?"

Walton stood there, as if listening. Watching.

"Walton!"

"Yeah. Yeah." Walton turned, shaking his head. The gravel crunched beneath his black running shoes. Walton hadn't run in years, perhaps a decade. He insisted that he keep them, just in case he needed to "chase down a perp, like I used to do."

Walton had caught precisely one suspect on foot in all his years on the force.

Rathford glanced back to the door. The door where darkness waited and his heart fluttered in his chest. He ducked into the vehicle, closed the door with a clap. Walton joined him a moment later, inserted the key, turned the vehicle over.

"Did you find anything?"

A shrug. "Dunno. I took video."

Walton smirked at him then glanced over his shoulder, backing them out. "You losing your edge? You always come back with something better than a lost jacket and some video."

Rathford sucked at his teeth and shifted in his seat, not looking at Walton. Gravel crunched under the wheels and Walton's smirk slowly faded.

"Walton."

A grunt.

"How long was I gone?"

Walton glanced at him, eyebrow raised, then back to the rear windshield. "I dunno. Twenty minutes? Thirty? Those woods ain't that thick."

Numbers flashed before his eyes. *00:66:66*

A chill swept from his heart to his palms.

"Yeah. Not that thick."

The car lurched as it shifted from reverse to drive. "Why?"

Rathford stared out the window at the empty house as it receded. The darkness seemed to watch them as they sped off.

"I think my phone needs a new battery."

A chuckle and Walton glanced at him, both hands on the wheel. "I know, right? Fuck Apple."

"Fuck Apple," Rathford murmured. He sighed, looking at Walton. "You got a charger?"

Lurker IV

The Lurker woke, air flooding his lungs, his eyes flashing open. There were—things—above him. More of them. More humans. More prey.

The wound in his chest throbbed, but it was swallowed up by the eager drumming in his veins. Unbidden, a vision of the screaming thing and its child, the smell of their fear, the snap of their bones. Yes, it was time to hunt again. Foolish creatures, drawn to the death of their own. His breath quickened, and he uncoiled, padding towards the spot of light at the far side of the chamber. He climbed the stepped slope on silent feet, his teeth clattering as he emerged into the grey light, eager to rip, to tear, to taste.

"—these make you wanna quit, don't they?"

A murmured reply and an electric pop, hiss, whine. The Lurker surmounted the incline into the chamber where he had first entered this place. The shattered crystal pane strewn across the floor, now populated with little yellow arches with glossy black markings. He pushed them aside, the bits of crystal squealing beneath his claws.

"I mean, I've been doing this for ten years, but—holy shit, I've never seen anything like this."

Another pop, hiss, whine, and the Lurker stepped closer, his teeth clattering louder. He knew, on some level, that they might hear him, hear the way his teeth clipped at the air, the rush of air in his lungs, the subtle growl in his throat, but that concern was small and far away. He felt his waking mind slip away; he needed this, needed to break them, slice them open, taste their final breaths, and so he trembled and clattered on, closer and closer.

"I mean, what kind of monster would do this? It's—inhuman. Like, *how* do you even do something like this?"

"I—I dunno, man. Just—let me take these pictures so we can get out of here." Pop, hiss, whine. A flash filled the portal between the chambers, filling the room where his victims lay. What were these simpletons doing? He almost laughed. All other things had the good sense to avoid the dead. The Lurker wrapped a long claw around the edge of the portal and peeked from behind the wall. Two humans. One kneeling, holding a large black contraption to his face, the other standing its back to the Lurker.

"Dave?"

A murmur from the kneeling one.

"Where's the kid's head?"

The kneeling one sighed and let the contraption fall away from its face. Slowly, it shook its head, raised a hand and ran it through its hair. "I dunno, man. I noticed that when we got in. Maybe we'll find it later on; we still got this whole damn house to comb through."

"You think the creep took it with him?"

"Maybe. Like the livers. Who knows with a case like this?" It raised the contraption to its face again, squinting.

The Lurker slid around the corner, breathless, teeth chattering in his skull. Oh, they were so close, so close he could taste them on the air. He could already feel them on his tongue.

"You hear that, Dave?"

"Hm?"

"It sounds like—sounds like someone's teeth are chattering."

The contraption dropped from the kneeling one's face again, and it tilted its head. "Now that you mention it—"

The Lurker was no more than two paces away from the standing one. It felt as though he couldn't get enough air, Shivers dashing up and down his limbs, along his spine. He raised up on his hind legs, stepping forward, breath afire in his throat, chest. So close. Oh yes. He opened his mouth, slowly inching towards the human's neck.

The kneeling human looked up and gasped, its eyes going wide as it fell backwards. The contraption it was handling flashed, and all went white, pain searing his eyes. The Lurker screamed, covering his face with his arms and falling back a step.

"What the actual—"

Damn these things, damn them and their stupid, simple contraptions! The Lurker howled and swung backhanded, connecting with something that gave way and hit to his right with a thud and a moan.

"Shit! Fuckshit sonofabitch what the fuck is fucking—"

The Lurker blinked and slowly the burning whiteness in his eyes faded and the chamber, blurry, returned to his sight. If that stupid human had done something permanent to his eyes, it would know such—

The human had its back to the wall, was fumbling with something at its waist, and the Lurker's breath caught. Just like the one who had wounded him when he first arrived. The device that blasted thunder and agony. The Lurker growled and dashed across the room, stepping on a corpse and sliding his claws into the human's chest between his bones. His vision cleared enough to see the thing's eyes go wide and its mouth fall open, croaking, gasping. It jerked and there was a thunderclap from the thing's waist, and the Lurker growled, sinking his claws deeper into the thing's chest. It whined, choking, and another thunderclap filled the chamber, leaving the Lurker's ears ringing. Then, a long gurgling sigh, blood from the mouth, and the eyes rolled back in its head. Death came so quickly to these little things. So easily they let go of their bodies and fled, but there was still time. He could see it, lingering in its hanging mouth, white and ephemeral. The Lurker turned his head and clamped his jaws around the thing's mouth and sucked. The body spasmed against the wall, kicking and jerking, and the Lurker sucked harder, wrenching the little soul from its tabernacle. It slid down his throat, filling his lungs, and the Lurker tipped his head back snapping his mouth shut. He let the body slide to the ground, now still and empty.

"Dave. God, you—you fucking—"

The Lurker turned, hunching, and saw the other human. He felt his lips peel back from his teeth. Laughter writhed in his throat and he stalked closer as it scrambled backward along the wall on palms and heels, dragging its ass along the floor.

Dave howled and thrashed in the back of his mind. *"Run! Run, Steve! Get the fuck out of here!"*

Steve whimpered, tears pouring from its face, breaths coming in quick, panicked gasps. Gods, these creatures were so easy to terrify. Loyal, though. Even as Dave struggled against him, the Lurker could sense that it was more for Steve's benefit than its own.

"Run, Steve!"

Steve fell backwards and landed on its back, eyes still locked on the Lurker. "Please. Please, I've got a wife. A kid. Please. Please, please—"

The Lurker stepped over it, one clawed hand on its chest, the other stroking its face, leaving lines of dribbling red as Steve mewed.

"Rrrrruuu—" The words, if the simple sounds could be called such, were strange in the Lurker's throat, his tongue. Brutal. Simplistic. Primitive.

"Get out of here!" Dave howled in the back of his mind.

"Rrruuunnnnn, Steve," the Lurker croaked.

Rathford VII

The drive was quiet. Not quite quiet enough. Walton kept trying to engage him in—something. Rathford could hardly concentrate. The possibilities of how the scene played out kept seeping into his mind. One way, then another. Each iteration progressively less plausible, but more gripping, more violent, more harrowing, as if his mind were dancing down the circles of hell.

They had still been warm when he got there. He shuddered. It was his fault they were dead. If he hadn't spent so long in the woods, hadn't lost himself in his own fucking delusions, they might still be alive.

Then the scene wormed into his temples again, how it might have played out before the perp had broken in and murdered them both. He'd always had a vivid imagination; it was his job, after all. Puzzle out the story of what happened. But sometimes his brain ran away with him, dragged him down into unpleasant dreams of gristle and death.

This was one of those times; he remembered the broken window and in his mind's eye he saw the woman smiling at her daughter, stroking her hair as the pancakes browned, and then the perp was behind her with a big fucking knife and—

Stop it.

Rathford scrubbed his face with one hand and stared out the window. Something was playing on the stereo. Something far away. But he couldn't hear it. He could tell it was playing, but he could feel the screaming in the back of his mind, his brain synthesizing what they probably sounded like in their last moments no matter how he tried to stop it. The screams filled his mind's ear, clawing through his skull to the point he could feel them pierce his actual eardrums, heedless of how he tried to push it back. His chest felt numb and empty and there was a claustrophobic pressure around his temples that made him want to curl up on the seat. He might have, if Walton hadn't been there.

Let the ghosts rest. Gotta find this psycho. Look at the evidence, work back from there. You don't know anything yet.

"You doing okay, man? You look pretty shook up."

The trees whizzing by were there. Some part of his mind recognized that, but that's not what he saw. Instead, he saw the killer smiling down at the woman, holding her by the neck as he plunged the knife into her stomach again and again while the girl screamed in the corner.

"Rathford, buddy."

The body of the headless child flashed through his mind and then he saw the murderer sawing at the child's neck with a butcher's knife while her mother pounded against his back, weeping, screaming.

"Hey!" There were fingers in front of Rathford's face, snapping again and again. He jerked and batted away the hand, then glared at Walton, who was glaring back.

"Don't you go fucking sideways on me now, man. You can do that when we're done with this crazy ass case."

Rathford's face burned and he ran a hand over it, then glanced at Walton. "I'm fine."

"You're not fine. You always do this when a case is getting to you."

He glared at Walton. "You don't know what you're talking about."

"Yeah? That Penny case." Walton took his hand from the wheel and lifted a finger. "The Cruz murders." Another finger. "The—"

"Fine! I get it!" Rathford threw his hands up. "Just—get us back to the precinct."

"Your car."

Rathford's brow furrowed and he looked at Walton for a moment before he shook his head and he looked away again.

"Fine, whatever. I just need—" He stopped, and looked

down at his hands. They were resting on his knees, palms up. What did he need?

He thought about it for a while and realized he didn't have an answer.

Walton just glanced at him and kept driving.

———

It took twenty minutes to get where his car was parked. The crime scene workers were just finishing up, some of them no doubt resentful that he'd asked them to stay in that dripping warehouse one second longer than they needed to. They didn't complain to him, though. If anything, he'd hear about it from the Chief or HR. He'd had that conversation before. Nothing ever came of it.

Walton watched him get out of the car and sat there, letting it idle, watching Rathford, who glanced back and gestured at the building. "I'm gonna have one more look around."

"Yeah. Sure, go ahead. What happened to your suit jacket?"

Rathford felt the tendons in his spine cinch, felt himself straighten. He glanced back at Walton. "It—got snagged in some branches when I was combing through those woods. Couldn't get it loose."

It wasn't a lie. But it was hardly the truth, either.

The truth will set you free.

Fat chance. More like the truth will get you locked in the madhouse for the foreseeable future.

Walton snorted and raised his eyebrow. "That's littering, you know. I could write you up for that."

A sparse chuckle escaped Rathford's mouth and a brief smile crossed his lips. "Yeah. You do that."

Walton laughed and waved. "See you back at base, man."

The passenger window rolled up and he drove off without looking back.

Rathford watched him pull out of the parking lot and accelerate down the road, then turned back to the warehouse. The smell had intensified, but there was something off that he couldn't put his finger on. Two men shuffled out of the building, a gurney between them with long black bags atop them. They murmured something he didn't quite catch.

"—more like bags of spare parts than body bags."

"Yeah, man. I felt like I was picking up doll parts after my son got into—"

The men hefted the gurney into the back of the ambulance and closed the doors. A moment later the engine rumbled to life and the lights flashed for a brief moment, then they too pulled out of the parking lot and were gone.

Rathford was alone once again.

He'd been alone many times in his life. In the vast expanse of the American Southwest where there had been a comforting, chilling awe. With his ex-wife as they'd yelled at one another, a cruel and crushing solitude. In the city as he stumbled home after a long night of drinking to his cold, dark apartment, and it felt as if he were adrift on a dark sea.

But this was new. As if he were trespassing on holy ground. For a heartbeat he had the urge to cast off his shoes, to avert his gaze, to flee. He could feel the skin on his back crawl, as if strange black eyes were watching him. He shrugged and a shiver ran down his spine, but he would not turn and look. He wouldn't.

Instead he walked toward the building, the smell of death crawling up his nose, worming its way into his brain. God, stop it. Nothing unusual. Bodies are bodies are bodies are bodies are —. He ran a hand over his lips. There were just more of them here. He ducked under the police tape and stepped into the scene, now devoid of human pieces, now littered with little yellow crime markers.

His footsteps sometimes echoed, sometimes not, instead peeling away from the coagulated muck. He felt bad on some level, but he saw other footprints among the sludge. Probably from the CSI unit. If even they hadn't been able to pick their way through the scene without disturbing anything, he had little chance of it.

The scene wasn't much different than the way he'd left it. The blood on the floor and the walls was becoming a pudding, and the stench had only intensified in the heat and the humidity. He swallowed and breathed through his mouth, but death hung so heavy in the air he could taste it. This was a bad idea. Should have let it sit a while. Come back with a respirator. Those usually kept most of the stink out.

He didn't know what he was looking for. Another reason he should have stayed away. No reason to haunt a scene when you didn't know what you were looking for. Look at it in the office, through pictures and descriptions and forensic evidence, come back when you had a theory to test. No reason to disturb the ghosts yet. Not until he had a working theory.

And yet, even with the stink, the shadows that seemed too dark, the persistent feeling of being watched—it was better than being alone with his thoughts. Here the ephemeral screams of the woman and her child were more distant. They didn't feel like they were burrowing into his skull just behind the ears.

Here it was just the scene, the evidence. It was a little gory, yes. Are the walls bleeding? No, it can't be. A little gloomy, even. It should not be this dark in here. It's nearly noon. And he couldn't shake the feeling of being watched. But it wasn't the worst scene he'd ever had to work.

Actually, it was. But it seemed like every other week a new scene claimed the title. He'd managed all the other ones just fine. This one would be no different. Big news, too, once the media shoved their dirty little noses where they didn't belong. Satanic cult. Ritualistic murders. Killer on the loose.

No way they'd keep a lid on this one. Especially not with the new scene.

If it bleeds, it leads, he thought wryly. Didn't matter that it would only cause a panic, that it tipped killers off more often than not, that it made his job a dozen times harder. The media always got their pound of flesh.

He walked, tracing the footsteps of the other investigators. Crime marker 1, 2, 3, 5. Seemed like the place was littered in them. Sometimes he could tell what they were meant to mark, often from the lack of the thing. The smear was shaped like an arm, a torso. Other times it was some item of inventory removed. What kind of warehouse was this? What did they store here? He didn't know. That might be relevant.

As he walked, something itched at the back of his mind. Not the screaming. That thought felt different in his mind. Breathless, claustrophobic, like his temples were being crushed in a vice. This was itchy, the feeling of a forgotten formula, or a dream just after waking as the eyes focused from that world to this one. He was missing something. He squatted down and tilted his head, looking at a crime marker that seemed apart from the rest of them. He rubbed his chin. What was it? What was he missing? This is why he came out to the scenes so often. To be alone, to connect with the scene, to frame it properly in his mind, to think where it was quiet instead of the constant buzz of the office—

He stopped and listened. That's what was missing. He stood, looked around. It was a warm, breezy day. Or it had been. Clouds had rolled in and the temperature felt like it had dropped ten degrees. He shivered and looked around the scene. Nothing moved, and the only sounds were those of his own breathing.

There were no flies.

Rathford VIII

It took Rathford the better part of an hour to get back to the precinct. He didn't remember most of the drive, too lost in his own thoughts to make much sense of anything. No flies. Why? How? Both of the crime scenes, now. Was it something the killer carried with him? Something coincidental? A bizarre detail. He knew it wasn't useful, such a small, stupid thing, but his mind wouldn't let go, and alternated like a pendulum between the screams of the slaughtered replaying over and over again in his mind and the strange restraint of the flies.

But there was the precinct. His home. Where he would get to the bottom of this, make things right. Not fix things; you could never do that. You can't put the people back into their family's lives or fill the holes in people's hearts, but you could make it right. Balance the scales.

There was a magpie sitting on the fence as he turned into the parking lot, and it took flight in a flurry of black, white, and iridescent blue as he passed it. Filthy birds. Entirely too smart for their own good, but it was strange to see one in the city like this. He thought they preferred more rural areas. Maybe they didn't. Maybe he'd just never noticed them before. He parked, got out of the vehicle, and stood there for a few heartbeats, a sense of unease resting just behind his ears, on his shoulder blades, on his spine. Even the city seemed too quiet. As if it knew something that the residents felt, but had not yet deduced. Maybe the media had already gotten ahead of him. The thought tugged the corners of his mouth down. He looked around the parking lot in the grey noon light, and saw another magpie. Or perhaps the same one. It watched him straight on, like a person might. On any other day he might not have even noticed it, but now it seemed to iconify the wrongness he felt as it watched him with those beady black eyes. He stared back at it, willing it to look away, to caw, or even move at all. It did not. Rathford broke the gaze, looking around for some small rock he could pitch at the animal, but he could find none and by the time he looked up again the magpie had taken wing, the coarse flaps echoing through the lot.

Rathford shook his head and stared after it for a moment or two, then walked into the precinct.

Fucking birds.

———

The precinct was a mess, like it always was. Too many people in and out, papers rustling, the drone of conversation, argument. More of the latter today. Rathford slipped between his coworkers to his desk at the back. There was a manila folder waiting for him and he flipped through the contents. Preliminary photos. Reports from the responding officers. Rathford had spoken with them himself, but maybe they would include something in these reports that they might have initially missed or things that they had meant to say but had lost like ravens on the wing. A quick glance at the reports confirmed what he already knew. Morning shift had found the scene, already hours old. A chaos of blood and entrails. Nothing new. Notes about body temperature put the time of the murders around midnight.

Hardly surprising, given the iconography and the mayhem involved.

Rathford passed over the photos. He already knew what they looked like, and the evidence wouldn't be logged and available for at least another few hours, if not another day or two depending on how much there was. Autopsies as well.

The morgue boys would be up late tonight.

He closed the folder and looked around the desk for the second scene. The horrified wails of child and mother tried to work its way forward in his brain, but he pushed them back to the dark corners of his mind. Not now. Not here. This is where I put it right.

But apparently the investigators hadn't gotten back yet. Hardly surprising. Work with what you've got. He opened the first folder and started to arrange the photos in a way that more or less matched the scene. This body here. That one there. Teenagers, by the look of it. Rich kids who smoked weed, tweeted about overthrowing the "system," and stayed out after dark just to irk their parents. A car, or several, that didn't belong to the warehouse were bound to be in the parking lot. He made a note to check the license plates later. Easier to track down the families that way, make more connections. But who would want to kill a bunch of fuckwitted teenagers?

By the time he'd finished with his collage, he saw the pattern emerging again. Attitudes of death that were too precise to be natural. A five pointed star with the poor security guard in the middle. Ritualistic, then? A safe enough conclusion, and his mind leapt to the well-dressed man who'd shown up at the loading bay, the man they'd riddled full of holes and left dead and grinning on the pavement. Had he been a part of it? Responsible, even?

You won't stop him, you know.

No, that made no sense. Rathford would have to check with the coroner for core body temps on the secondary victims for a more-precise timeline, but the man in the suit was at the primary scene at around the same time that the murders at the second scene were probably happening. And he had the feeling that the actual killer wouldn't steal an officer's sidearm when he'd gone through so much trouble to slice up the other victims like he had.

Still, the well-dressed man was an irritating loose end. Seemed to know what was going on. Or, at least, he thought he did. He could very well be some poor fool having a psychotic break. Stranger things had happened.

You won't stop him, you know.

What was his name? Not included in the file. Goddamn it, Steve. That should have been the first thing on the report. How hard was it to pull a driver's license out of a man's back pocket? He ran a hand over his face. If Steve didn't pull his shit together—

Not his business. His business was tracking down this psycho as quick as possible. Seems like the fucker wanted to burn like a stick of dynamite, and Rathford was *not* going to let that happen.

Eight. That's all you get, asshole.

You won't stop him.

That man's words, his reckless smile, refused to be pushed out of Rathford's head. Even as his eyes wandered over the other evidence, the nameless man pushed into his mind again and again. There was something there. He knew something. Had known something. The way the corpse had looked at him, grinned, even as they loaded him in the ambulance, blood leaking from between the teeth—

No. Muscle spasms. This was *not* a fucking zombie flick.

Again Rathford tried to focus on what he had on his desk, but he could almost feel the nameless man behind him, his spine ramrod straight, hands clasped behind his back, that Cheshire grin on his face, looking down at him, mocking him.

Puny little man. You won't stop him. You can't stop him. He cannot be stopped. Any more than a hurricane or a volcano. He is come to snatch the light from the sky and gnaw the life from your bones. He is—

Fuck it. Rathford grabbed his phone. The fucking businessman was as good a place as any to start. He probably wouldn't give him any real clues, but maybe it would get him to shut the fuck up. And he was the only piece of the case that didn't have the feel of random, mindless violence, the only thing that felt like it pointed anywhere. He queued up Steve's number and put the phone to his ear.

It rang.

And rang.

And rang.

Then it went to voicemail. Goddamn it, Steve. Rathford called again, and the same thing happened, but now something cold wormed around behind his sternum. He might let one call go unanswered, but two?

Rathford called a third time. Still it rang, and rang on long after it should have gone to voicemail again, and Rathford's throat went dry.

"Walton. How long was I gone?"

"I dunno. Twenty, thirty minutes? Those woods ain't that thick."

00:66:66

He stood and grabbed for the jacket that should have been

draped over the back of his chair but was not. Walton was standing over a colleague's desk, a manilla folder in his hand, and he looked up at Rathford as he stood.

"You goin' somewhere?"

Steve and Dave are in trouble.

"I'm gonna go see if Steve and Dave are done."

Walton raised his wrist and looked down at his watch. "You sure? They ain't gonna be done for another hour at least."

Rathford shrugged. "Maybe they can use another hand."

Walton held his eyes for a long moment, then shrugged too and looked away. "Alright. Just don't get too sticky."

Rathford wanted to smile. Wanted to make some snide, morbid joke, but nothing came. His mind was blank. Or rather, it was too full of the images of the dead, the screams of the dying.

"Yeah," he croaked.

Rathford IX

Rathford felt like he couldn't breathe. Like his airway wasn't wide enough or his lungs weren't deep enough. The AC was on high, yet sweat dripped down his face, and the steering wheel creaked under his grip.

Round and round he goes, where he stops, nobody knows!

None of his other cases had ever felt like this, not even the most gruesome. There was always an urgency, yes, but not like this. Eight deaths in as many hours. With other killers there was time to gather evidence, time to lay traps, or do surveillance before he struck again, if he struck again.

This guy didn't even give you time to think.

Eight. That's all you get, motherfucker.

But his gut told him he was wrong. It told him he was already too late.

He was coming up on another vehicle, and Rathford contemplated flashing his lights, but instead he pursed his lips and pressed on the brake pedal. It was a long, lonely two-lane highway, and though the oncoming traffic was sparse, it was enough that he couldn't just fly around the vehicle in front of him like he'd done with the last three cars.

They're fine. You're being paranoid. Just because the phone's being fucky doesn't mean —

The steering wheel creaked under his grip.

Doesn't mean what? Doesn't mean they're having the flesh peeled slowly off their bones? There was one like that. Or maybe they'll have their eyes sucked out and their tongues bitten off like that girl. Or maybe they'll just have their entrails—

Rathford rubbed a hand over his face and took a deep, deep breath, then held it for one, two, three, four, five, and let it slowly out his nose.

They're fine.

There was a break in the oncoming traffic, and Rathford slammed down his accelerator. The woman in the driver's seat looked over at him as he passed, and he thought he saw surprise on her face for the heartbeat that their eyes met, but then she was behind him.

A few minutes later his phone buzzed. He grabbed it and glanced at the screen. Walton. What the hell did he want? He put it to his ear.

"What do you need, Walton?"

"We're getting reports of a reckless driver on I-80. Is that you?"

Rathford glanced down at the speedometer. Ninety-five. He sighed.

"Might be."

"Goddamn it. Either turn your lights on or slow the fuck down. We do not need this right now."

Walton hung up before Rathford could say any more, and Rathford hurled the phone into the passenger seat, then reached for the switch to turn on his lights.

They're fine. You're being paranoid.

His hand froze and he stared at the switch for a long moment, lips pursed.

You're being paranoid.

The woods from earlier flashed through his mind with the cloying dark, the twisting path of the murderer, the way his phone battery ticked down before his eyes.

You're being paranoid.

He sighed and leaned back in his seat, slowly putting pressure on the brake pedal.

———

When he pulled up to the house there were two other vehicles in the driveway—the victim's and the forensic team's. He parked his car and watched the house. Nothing moved, except the storm above. The clouds were dark and angry, and thunder rolled now and again, but he saw no lightning and no raindrops fell, and the crime scene tape fluttered in the wind like an abandoned ribbon.

Something was wrong, but he did not yet know what it was. Or rather, perhaps it was just the conjunction of things. The storm that rose too quickly and dropped only thunder. The chill wind. The way the house was dark and quiet. Dave and

Steve weren't the type to work in the dark, or even turn the lights off when they left the room.

All of these things could have been ignored on their own, but the way they danced together now made Rathford's shoulders crawl together, made his heart beat lightly, quickly in his chest. The rising unease he'd felt at the precinct settled into his lungs now, making it hard to breathe.

He watched the house, watched the windows. A light breeze rippled across his skin as he watched, making his hair stand on edge and a shiver run down his spine. Nothing moved. He should have seen *something* move. Seen someone come out. Seen anything at all, but it was like trying to peer through dark water at midnight.

He grabbed his phone off the passenger seat and slipped it into his pocket as he climbed out of the car.

Something tittered behind his ear. Something primal. The same thing that had told him not to follow the trail earlier that morning. The rising hairs on the back of his neck. The feeling of being watched. The absolute silence.

As he walked up to the front door, the feeling grew stronger, each step echoed in his ears and he felt more and more like a rabbit walking into a bear den. The door was still ajar, a dent near the handle where his heel had landed and the frame in a fray of splinters. But even with the door wide open, Rathford found he could not see inside the house.

He looked up. The clouds roiled and rumbled above him. He swallowed and looked down again, rubbing the gun he hadn't realized he'd grabbed.

"Steve? Dave? You guys in there?"

The question felt small, flat, stupid. Of course they were. Where else would they be? Even if they'd gone to get food or some stupid shit like that, the car would be gone and—

"Dave? Steve?"

He climbed the first step, the second, the third, and was standing on the landing before the front door, but he still could not see inside.

Just blackness.

He called louder. "Dave. Steve."

A coarse, harsh laugh came from inside.

"Rathford."

Rathford's heart leapt in his chest and he scrambled backwards down the front steps. He heard another laugh and for a moment he thought he saw the white of long dead bone and a glimpse of eternal fire. His heart lodged itself in his throat, rattled in his ears, but he swallowed it down and placed his foot on the first stair.

"Guys?"

"They." The word was labored, as if formed on the lips of one unused to speaking. "Are here."

"Who? Who's there?" He already knew the answer to the question, but he couldn't help but ask it.

"David. Steeeeven."

Rathford opened his mouth again to speak, but before any sound escaped another word came from the darkened doorway, one that chilled his bones.

"Rathford," the grim, grinding voice called again.

His breath felt cold inside his lungs, and he felt his hand raising the pistol, finger brushing the trigger, though he had no target to point at.

"What did you do to them." It should have been a question, but it wasn't.

"Ate. Them." A long, shuddering breath, chattering teeth. "Delicious."

Rathford's lips curled and his hands tightened around his

weapon. He raised it at the yawning dark that lurked inside the door.

"Come out. Come out with your hands up."

Another guttural laugh. "Come in."

Rathford gritted his teeth and peeled back his lips, pistol trained on the door, weight shifting from one foot to the other. He did not want to go in there. If he had another officer—or two or ten or fifty—he might try it. But by himself? Against a murderous cannibal—*monster?* That was a bad idea for a hundred different reasons.

"I'll shoot."

A hiss and a rustle. "Lead will not stop me."

"You wanna make a fucking bet? Because I've got a bullet with your name on it, pal."

The man —*the monster*— inside laughed at him. "I know your name, *Rathford.* You know not *mine.*"

A shudder rippled down his throat and he took a step back when Rathford heard his own name.

"Michael Rathford. Powerful name. It will not save you."

A shiver ran down his spine and his ribs felt cold. My name's Charlie, not Michael. But the name slid over him like it belonged to him, like it had always been his.

"What's a fucking name got to do with it?"

"Everything."

Rathford's hands trembled, but he kept his pistol pointed at the door. "Look, pal. You can come out now or I can call the SWAT team. Your choice."

The thing behind the dark laughed, and from the way the voice echoed, Rathford thought it had turned away.

"Begone, little magpie. Before I taste you, too."

With that, Rathford's phone buzzed in his pocket and he

jumped as if he'd been stung, looking briefly down, then back up at the bleak doorway.

"Hey! Hey, come back here! I ain't done with you yet!"

The dark house was silent. Nothing moved. Nothing breathed. Not even Rathford. The only sound in that place was the phone vibrating against his leg.

"This ain't over!" he shouted, a sound that died away without echo and without response. His phone fell still in his pocket and the wind stirred again, and the foxtail seemed to whisper things to him, things he could not quite make out.

He opened his mouth, but before he could say anything his phone buzzed again. He swore under his breath and dug the device out of his pocket, juggling firearm and phone and keeping his eye on the house, the fields, the sky.

"Rathford."

"Fucking god, I've been trying to reach you for half an hour. Get your ass back here now. And bring our two prima donnas with you."

"Wha—what the hell are you talking about? I got the killer right here but—"

"You have him in custody?"

"Not him. It. It's here. But I don't—"

"So, it was an animal? Well, I've got two dead EMTs dumped on the side of Fifth and Main and a missing ambulance. Get back here now. And bring Dave and Steve. I don't care if you have to stick them in your fucking clown car, just get back here."

Rathford's mouth and throat went dry and he looked up at the broken door and the velvet black beyond. He could smell the blood, fresh spilled and old alike.

"Dave and Steve are," he swallowed sand. "Dave and Steve are dead."

There was a long pause and Rathford could hear the foxtail rustle.

"Jesus fucking Christ. Just—" A sigh. "Just get back here."

The line went dead and Rathford held the phone to his ear, his eyes wide and unseeing, his mouth open. After a moment, his hand closed tighter around the cool metal and glass and he had to stop himself from pitching it into the house.

"I'll be back!" he shouted. "I'll be back, and I'm gonna—I'm gonna." Tears clouded his eyes, and he turned away. He took the first step when he heard the voice again, and it stopped him in his tracks.

"Foolish child. I will not be here. The dark comes."

Rathford looked back and saw a pair of eyes in the dark, burning white. As he watched, the bare muzzle of some long dead predator slipped into the light and began to smoke subtly. The muzzle lifted and the eyes, like callous stars, turned upward, and Rathford followed them.

Above the house, the clouds swirled and darkened. Already the gloom was deepening. Lightning flashed from one cloud to another and it blinded him for a moment. While he was blinking away the searing white from his eyes, the thunder rolled through his flesh, through his bones, and pushed him back a step. When he could hear again, he heard laughing coming from the house. He looked up and saw the skull with the burning eyes staring at him.

"I see you, Rathford."

The words sent a chill through his bones and his gut contracted, but instead of cowering, Rathford sneered. "I see you too, motherfucker."

He raised the pistol and fired one-handed.

A cheekbone shattered, and a large piece flew smoking through the air. The creature screamed and disappeared, but

Rathford fired again. And again. And again. He fired until the pistol locked open and the last brass casing fell to the pavement with a rattling chime.

For a long moment, nothing moved. Not the clouds, not the thing in the house, not Rathford himself. The whole world seemed to still. Then Rathford slowly exhaled and lowered his weapon. Still nothing moved.

What the fuck was going on?

He wiped the cold sweat from his brow with the back of his left hand, and found it trembling, still wrapped around his phone. Another deep breath and slowly the tremors stopped. He glanced up at the door again. A few of his shots had gone wide. Very wide. He could see the bullet holes on either side of the door, and one of the anchor points for the crime scene tape had come undone, leaving it fluttering in the wind like a long ribbon. A moment later and it came lose completely, sailing into the sky like an eel.

He should call it in. Officer-involved shooting—at what? No one would ever believe him. He didn't believe himself. He scrubbed his face and turned back to his car, the smell of burnt gunpowder filling his nose.

Behind him, tangible darkness began to seep from the doorway like cold smoke creeping across the ground. It poured over the landing, down the sides, down the steps. Rathford pulled out his spare magazine and cursed. Empty. He'd emptied it this morning on the grinning man they'd put in the ambulance. He thumbed the slide release and even as the pistol snapped closed, long claws slipped through the door and wrapped around the frame, smoking. A heartbeat later, the long dead skull crept out, the muzzle and teeth beginning to smoke as well. The rest of the skull soon followed, now bereft of a cheekbone, bleak white stars burning in the eye sockets, and two small antlers cradling a pair of pulsing white orbs. The long jaw trembled and the gleaming teeth chattered.

Perhaps it was chance that saved Rathford. Perhaps he heard something. Perhaps it was instinct, perhaps a subtle whisper from on high. Regardless, Rathford looked over his shoulder while he was sliding his pistol back into its holster and saw the thing creeping through the door. The creature of bleached bone, of claws, of black sinew and black, bristly fur.

It screamed, the long hackles rising, and launched itself through the air, claws outstretched.

Rathford dropped, falling on his ass as he felt the whoosh of air overhead, and the thing landed, the long claws tearing long furrows in the grass as it scrabbled and turned to face him. The whole thing smoked in the sparse sunlight and stank like sulfur, he noticed as it found traction on the grass, spun, and leapt at him again. He dove to the side, landing hard and knocking the wind out of his lungs, but hardly noticed as he pushed himself to his feet and ran to his car.

The thing pounded after him, growling, snapping, and for a heartbeat he was glad that he'd lost his suit coat earlier that morning, as he could hear the claws slicing through the long air mere inches behind him. He leapt and slid across the hood on his hip, chancing a look over his shoulder. The creature reached out over the hood of the car and slashed at him, the long claws whistling through the air. For a heartbeat he thought the beast had missed completely, but time seemed to still when he saw the scattered droplets of deep, dark red hanging in the air in an arc, and then his feet hit the ground, the asphalt slipping under his soles, his own balance teetering as the damned thing clambered up over the hood of his car, the claws, *more like foot-long knives*, slipping across the paint in a scrabble of squealing steel.

Rathford stumbled forward, reached out and grabbed the driver-side handle. The creature screamed at him and raised one clawed hand. He ducked, still pulling the door open, and felt the claws slice through the air above him, then watched the creature overbalance and tumble sideways, landing flat on its back on the asphalt.

Rathford jumped into the car and slammed it shut behind him, hand digging in his pocket for the keys even as the thing rolled to its feet and charged at him again. It slammed into the car and the car rocked, shocks squealing.

I'm safe. Whatever the fuck that thing is, there's no way it can—

The thing bit at the door, one tooth finding purchase between window and frame, and yanked. The door squealed and bent, the window instantly shattering into a spider web of cracks. A shock ran through Rathford and he slammed the key into the ignition and turned the car over. It sputtered for a moment, as if the battery were nearly dead, and the frame bent even more, to the point that Rathford could see a sliver of sky beyond and feel the fetid breath of the creature heaving through the gap. He turned the engine over again and heard the same whining, sputtering, and another squeal as the door frame bent further. Bits of broken glass tinkled to the ground, and the long claws of the thing stabbed through the gap between door and car and yanked. The whole vehicle rocked and squealed, the door bending further.

Rathford's heart leapt into his throat and he scrabbled over the center console into the passenger seat, hand groping blindly for the handle. But instead of the handle, his hand found something smooth, cold, hard. He glanced at it.

His hand was wrapped around the barrel of his shotgun. He hit the lock and yanked it free, swinging the butt up to his shoulder just as the creature tore the door free of his car and tossed it across the road. It ducked into the car as he was sliding his forefinger into the trigger guard, the long claws tearing into the seat with hardly any effort at all, but it froze when it saw the barrel of the twelve-gauge pointed right at its face.

"What was that about you and lead?"

The creature screamed and its hackles rose, but as it lurched forward he thumbed off the safety and fired.

The blast made Rathford's ears ring and his vision swim like he'd been knocked in the jaw, but the creature reeled back. He was sure it must be screaming, but he could hardly hear it as it stumbled, holding its face with both claws.

It should be dead. Not even a bear can take a twelve-gauge to the face.

But it was not. When the long claws came away from the face, Rathford could see the skull was pocked with smears of lead, but the cold white eyes burnt just as bright as before. The long jaw unhinged and Rathford felt rather than heard the scream that followed.

He racked the pump and fired again and again, the recoil slamming his shoulder against the passenger door with each pull of the trigger, but the creature stumbled back with each shot. Then the trigger clicked and no fire came.

Smoke curled in the cab of the car and the stench of burnt gunpowder seared Rathford's nose, but the creature still stood, panting, smoking, about halfway across the road.

Fuck me.

The creature looked up and locked eyes with Rathford, the hackles rising again, but Rathford didn't wait to see if it had the energy for another charge. He jumped over the center console and turned the key. This time the car roared to life, so he slammed it into gear and stomped on the gas, the lurch pushing him back into his seat. He fishtailed for a moment, heart rolling from side to side in his chest as he fought the steering wheel, nearly tumbling out of the car, but soon the car straightened and he was off. He looked into the rear view mirror, and he saw the thing in the middle of the road, smoking, screaming at him even as he sped off down the highway.

By the time Rathford got back to the precinct, his ear and face were aching and the left side of his shirt was drenched dark red and sticky, and his whole left side was numb from the buffeting winds of his drive.

He didn't remember most of it. He remembered the— thing. Whatever it was. And he remembered when he entered the city proper because he actually had to remove his foot from the accelerator and use the brake, at which point he realized he'd been riding the redline the entire way back. Normally, a cold thrill would have run through his chest, but he felt nothing. In some distant way he realized he was in shock, but in that same distant way, he realized he didn't fucking care.

There was a goddamn monster on the loose, one that could rip the doors off cars and take six rounds of buckshot to the face.

But the rest of the trip was a blur, and now he was pulling into the precinct parking lot. It felt surreal to pull into one of the stalls, almost as surreal as unbuckling his seatbelt and stepping out of the gaping hole that had once had a door.

Rathford swayed when he stood, blackness rising at the back of his vision, so he reached out and grabbed the hood of the car. When he could see again, he noticed a sharp pain in his fingers. He looked down and saw his fingers bleeding over the ragged sheet metal where the thing's teeth must have torn it. His hand turned over, seemingly of his own accord, and he was suddenly fascinated by the dark, dripping blood making its way idly over his hand.

"Rathford. Rathford, buddy. Holy fuck. What the hell happened out there? We called you on the radio, on the phone, everything. You okay?"

Rathford felt a hand on his shoulder and he heard Walton's voice, and when he looked up he saw Walton's face pale and wide eyed. He'd heard the words that his friend was saying, but when he tried to make sense of them it was like grabbing smoke. So instead he extended his bleeding hand, palm upturned, like a child might.

"Okay. Yeah. Okay, buddy. We'll get that taken care of. Don't you worry." Walton patted him on the back and Rathford looked back down at his hand, watching the blood twist and turn, following the creases in his palm. Blood follows the heart line, he thought idly.

"Get me a fucking ambulance, now!" Walton shouted.

Rathford felt Walton's hand shift on his back, pushing him even as he shouted. He felt his feet stutter forward. He heard other exclamations as if they came through water. Through it all he watched the blood drip from his hand, leaving dark, red speckles on the blacktop as he walked.

Walton sat him down on the steps to the precinct, and a few moments or minutes or hours later, Rathford felt a blanket being wrapped around his shoulders. He heard words like, "Shock," and, "hit and run."

What kind of hit and run leaves a car frame bent outward instead of in?

"Wasn't a hit and run," he felt himself mutter. It felt strange. His eyes were unfocused and his mind was still empty save for the lead-streaked skull of the creature that had torn the door off his car.

The video. He had the video.

The video proved nothing.

"Huh?" Walton glanced over his shoulder at him.

He felt his neck turn and his eyes focused on Walton's. "It wasn't a hit and run."

Walton chuckled once, his eyes breaking from Rathford's and glancing over the wreck of the car. "What do you mean? What else could it a'been?"

A half dozen thoughts flashed through Rathford's head.

Lead will not stop me.

They'll never believe you.

Begone, magpie.

This ain't a fucking zombie flick.

I will not be here.

Six rounds of buckshot.

I know your name, Rathford. You know not mine.

That final thought echoed in his mind, culling all the others. His pulse quickened, and he swore he could see his breath rising in the warm summer air.

"I dunno. But it knows my name."

9

The Perpetual

Tim Keller

JACE LEFT the bar when they started with the horror stories. There hadn't been but a handful of customers all night, and Mickey evidently hadn't had enough Halloween. He'd started in with some pretty intense stuff, all of which he swore had really happened to his "roommate's ex-girlfriend's dad" or his "brother's boss's sister."

Jace hated scary stories. Always had, even back in scouts. Baby Beau and Mickey never seemed to get scared, but Jace couldn't help empathizing with the characters—characters who invariably became victims.

A hand fell on his shoulder as he grabbed the door handle.

"Don't leave!" Beau said.

Jace rolled his eyes and shrugged. "You know I hate that scary stuff."

"They're not that bad. Big Jim's the one with the really freaky ones."

Jace glanced across the bar at the club's bouncer. Jim

flashed him a knowing smile, mischievous and only slightly evil, the smile that softened his nearly seven-foot presence. Jim was good people and always looked out for the boys. But his sense of humor was as dark as his ebony skin, and tonight Jace could tell the tales had only just begun; if he stayed, it would be a long night indeed.

"Nah," he said. "Gotta work."

"Seriously?" Beau said. "It's bad out there. You should stay."

"Don't worry about me," Jace said, stepping out. "I'll be fine."

It was a long walk to the bridge, especially with the north wind blowing down a storm. An MTA bus rumbled toward him. There was a stop right in front of the bar, but that meant two transfers and at least an hour out of his way; plus he was down to his last five. If he walked, he could at least eat, even if business was slow.

Wind whistled through the concrete canyons and tore at the alleyways and storefronts. There was nothing between Jace's skin and the elements save a ripped pair of designer jeans, a skin-hugging tank-top, and a denim jacket.

Can't work a place like the XES Lounge dressed like Nanook of the North.

Jace pulled his jacket collar up a little higher, shivering against the wind and cursing his decision to stay in the city when the others had headed south.

Less competition equals more money.

But on nights like this one, the cold was a double-edged sword, keeping both hustler and john off the streets. The street light over the bus stop blew out, raining sparks like a hundred shooting stars and plunging the street into darkness. Jace shivered again, this time not from the cold.

There was no one in sight, and yet he couldn't shake the feeling that someone was out there. Mickey called it a "gift," and in this profession, a handy one. Anytime, anywhere, even in the dark, if a set of eyes so much as glanced in Jace's direction, he knew it, felt it. Good for business, and for giving muggers the slip. Beau, on the other hand—a whole stadium could be staring at Beau and he'd be oblivious. Some people just couldn't develop the skill.

They were the ones who didn't last long, the ones who disappeared without a trace.

That's why we have to watch out for Beau.

Jace stopped. Staring into the storefront windows, he scanned the reflection in the glass for movement. Nothing.

Probably those jerks from the bar. Well, if I can't see them, they can't see me.

A taste of their own medicine might do them some good. Jace darted into an alley, sprang onto a dumpster and crouched to wait.

Minutes ticked by as the cold, hardly slowed by his jacket, seeped into his bones.

"Fuck this!" he hissed, sliding off the dumpster. "You hear me?" he shouted. "I'm not playing anymore!"

His voice was snatched away on the whistling wind, and for a heartbeat he wasn't sure he'd shouted at all. Upon receiving no response, Jace peeked warily into the street. The empty street—empty, in the city that never sleeps, nothing in sight but blowing debris in the distant glow of still-functioning street lamps.

"Bad drugs," he reasoned aloud, rubbing his face. "No more after-parties for me." But the words sounded anemic and shrill. He felt an inexplicably immense sense of disapproval; as though he'd sworn in church—or worse—as though something better left to slumber might wake.

He stared down the sidewalk for the span of a few more heartbeats, then turned, hunched his shoulders and walked into the wind again. The only other sounds were the wind and his hurried footfalls on the pavement.

That he walked this way all the time should have been reassuring. He knew every building, alley, and sidewalk crack, but tonight the half-lit street was full of shadows that seemed as if they might at any moment solidify and come to life. It felt more like an alien facsimile than the street he knew. A parade of spiders wandered up his spine. This was more than just the jitters—something was wrong. Jace couldn't see it, or hear it, but something stalked him. He swallowed hard and walked faster, looking up to check his progress against the distant lights, yet he never seemed to gain.

Then he did hear it—faint echoes bouncing toward him from the darkness. For a moment he thought his heart might explode. Then he recognized the sound.

Footsteps, he reasoned. *Just a man, and only one at that, some old troll hoping for a freebie, no doubt. Well, he can have it. He can be Quasi-fuckin-modo for all I care. If it gets me out of here, I'll show him the time of his fucking life.*

"Hey," Jace called, "anybody there?"

Silence.

"Come on, man," he challenged with considerably more bravado than he felt. "I hear you back there. Come out and maybe we can party."

A man stepped from the shadows, impossibly close.

Tall, middle-aged, could use a little more on his head and a little less around the middle. Almost handsome, but for a rictus grin and a strange tilt to his head.

I've definitely done worse.

The man approached.

"So—you got a place?"

Silence.

"I don't see a car," Jace observed. "Hey, s'all good, ya know? I mean, whatever, just, can we get going? Kinda cold out here."

The man suddenly seized Jace by the arm, his grip like a vice, and drew him inexorably close. He smiled through full, sensuous lips—wider than should have been possible—and licked Jace's cheek with the tip of a grotesquely long tongue, a gesture simultaneously voluptuous and repellent. Jace might have taken that in stride but for the eyes, obsidian orbs that reflected his own dismayed face.

"Uhh," Jace stammered. "I don't think—I mean, sorry dude, maybe some other night, okay?"

The smile spread wider. "Tell me, little one," he said, "how would you prefer to die?"

"I'm not going to die," Jace replied, squirming, his free hand fingering the switch from its hiding place. He'd dealt with psychos before.

"You all die."

"Not me," Jace replied evenly.

The man threw back his head and laughed, revealing a mouth full of fangs. His breath smelled of rotting meat. "And just how do you intend to prevent it? By appealing to my better nature?"

The boy's arm swung in a tight arc, burying the blade in the man's ribcage. Jace's ferocity surprised even him.

"I'm not going to die, you asshole!" he screamed, driving the man back with the plunging blade.

Again and again he stabbed, blood spraying, gushing over his hand. Then they were tumbling backwards, the man's hand still so tight around Jace's arm that he thought he felt his bones creaking.

He kept stabbing, burying his knife in the man's ribs again and again as he—it—writhed and squirmed beneath him. He stabbed until the man's grip tightened, then loosened, then finally fell away. When the man stopped twitching, Jace rose—bloody and quivering—turned, and lurched away.

Wisps of steam rose from the blood on his face and hands. Steam rising like spirits leaving the earth.

The cops will never believe me.

Exhausted, he ducked into an alley way and collapsed against a wall behind some boxes. He'd killed a man.

That was no man.

Mickey! The thought jumped into his head. Mick would know what to do. He fumbled his phone from his pocket. The screen was cracked but to his great relief it powered up. The words *no service* mocked him from the upper right corner of the screen.

Text, then.

Jace had read or maybe heard somewhere that even when calls wouldn't go through, texts might. He'd heard the numbers one in three, but his mind felt gummy, foggy, flashes of the man's teeth, his grip, his blood jolting through his brain. His thumbs flashed over the keys, then stopped, and cleared. What if the cops got hold of it? His or Mickey's.

He jumped at the sound of footsteps behind him but stayed hidden. It had to be a beat-cop, that or some silly do-gooder with a hero complex.

"Fuck me!" he hissed. Again his fingers flew, almost as fast as his randomly firing synapses: *in trouble! 911! should have stayed, sorry!*

But the moment he touched the *send* button, the phone

erupted into sparks and a plume of caustic smoke. Jace stared dumbfounded at the mass of smoldering plastic on the ground, until the screen lit up.

I see you

He chanced a single glance into the street.

Little one

Jace ran then, so fast his feet felt like they might break free and escape on their own.

It was only when he stopped to catch his breath that he heard it, the lazy, almost tuneless whistle of a man without a care in the world.

Terror leapt from Jace's control, no longer a known commodity, no longer calling for a rational response. Primal it was, the fear of ancient ancestors being stalked in the jungle night.

Jace faltered—then broke, racing blindly through the deserted labyrinth of streets and alleys. Fear skewed everything. The buildings, the streets, they all looked alike. He didn't even know where he was anymore. Hoping to find a cop, person, any sign of life at all, Jace made a quick turn, thinking he'd finally found a street but ran headlong into a wall. Jace turned to go back, but the man stepped into the mouth of the alleyway. The stranger smiled, the predatory smile of a hunter who had cornered his prey after an amusing chase. Predatory and cold, much colder than the wind. Icy needles stabbing into Jace's heart.

It lowered its head, looking at him as a lover might as the jaw fell open and seemed to unhinge to reveal row after row of those jagged teeth, like long, serrated blades.

Jace tried to scream but managed only a strangled moan. *This can't be happening, can't be real.* He sank to his knees as the man advanced.

"You didn't answer my question," it said.

He felt it then, a familiar presence, a sensation not unlike that of coming in from the cold. Sudden, strong, and—not alone—like plugging into a socket, a surge of power coursed through him. Jace rose and drew his blade.

"Yes—I—did."

The stranger heard it then, the sound of another set of footsteps in the alley behind him, then another, and another. The smile on the thing's face evaporated into a feral snarl as Big Jim, his trusty baseball bat in hand, flanked by Mickey with a length of rebar and Beau holding a brick, stepped under the glow of a now-functioning street light.

"Better run, motherfucker," Jim snarled in his bouncer voice, deep and harsh: the authoritarian tone of a man accustomed to being obeyed.

"Fools—" it snarled, but the brick was already in the air, tumbling and slamming right into his eye.

"Leave him alone you fucking psycho!" Beau screeched.

The thing stumbled back, hand going to his face. Just as it straightened, Jim stepped in, snarling, and swung like Babe Ruth for the cheap seats, catching the thing in the cheek and snapping his head back.

The thing charged Beau but received only a blinding blast of Mickey's mace for his trouble. This deflected most of what would surely have shattered Beau like fine crystal. Then, between the blink of one eye and the next—Jim was there. Placing itself between Jim and the others, it whirled around, catching Jim in a deadly pirouette. Just as Jim lost the battle to stay on his feet, Jace waded, slashing, into the fray.

Beau, having picked up his brick, became the new target. He cocked his arm. "Come on!" he shouted, his call devolving to a battle cry.

Jace and Jim fell in beside him. The air crackled with energy as they advanced, their attacker now prey. Then, perhaps for the first time ever, it ran. Not far, not even fast, more to regroup than retreat, taking refuge in the shadows between street lamps. It spun and snarled, wicked teeth gleaming, the wind snapping its now ragged clothes.

"You could never have saved him," it snarled, "nor now even yourselves. You're all just a smorgasbord to me."

To which Mickey dropped his rebar and lifted his shirt to pull out his derringer and blow two smoking holes in its chest. It screamed, stumbling back, clutching itself as blood ran through its fingers and plipped onto the pavement.

Then it looked up. "You shouldn't have done that."

It was on them before Jace could blink, backhanding him across the chest. He flew into the wall, head cracking against the bricks and wind driven from his lungs. Dazed and barely able to breathe, Jace could only watch as the man-thing flattened Big Jim. It seized Jim's bat like a trophy and snapped it in two.

Mickey was trying desperately to reload the tiny pistol. Beau's brick smashed again and again against the thing's head until it backhanded Beau and sent him flying twenty feet. Hot tears welled up behind Jace's eyes.

So close, he thought.

But he couldn't lose his friends, too. Jace howled his frustration, which to his amazement stopped the thing mid-step. It staggered, as if physically struck, for seconds only, but it was enough.

Jim charged the thing, now swinging fists. Jace had seen firsthand the damage those fists could do, keeping the thing off balance long enough for Jace to push himself to his feet. He charged and buried his blade in the thing's throat. The thing screamed, turned its head, and snapped at Jace.

Jace snarled back through gritted teeth, twisting the blade. Then he heard a pair of pops behind him, and he felt something hit his arm.

"Shit!" Mickey said. "Sorry."

As Jace fell away, he thought, *Weird, it didn't even hurt all that much.*

But it was enough for the thing to throw him off. Jace landed on his tailbone, a shock running up his spine, and then he watched as it slammed its fist into Jim's chest so hard Jim flew back and skidded on his back for a dozen feet. Next it raised its chin and scowled, grabbed the handle of the knife and ripped it out, then turned and advanced on Jace, its black eyes locked on his.

A much louder shot split the night, and the thing's head exploded, showering Jace with blood and fragments of bone. The body stiffened, twin spouts of blood pulsing from the stump of the neck. It fell to its knees, then splatted forward, the blood pooling as the fountains pulsed.

A man in body armor stepped into the alley, carrying a gun so big it looked like a cannon.

"Fuckers are like zombies," he said. "Gotta hit 'em in the head or they just keep coming."

Two black sedans and a van screeched to a halt in the street, from which several men clad in black body armor and helmets emerged. They shoved Jace and the others into the far corner of the alley.

Jace watched in shock as the largest of the men produced a backpack mounted with two metal tanks and a nozzle on a hose. With this contraption, he drenched the corpse with a stream of ignited fuel. The wind had stopped, and the flames rose in the night, lighting the buildings with orange light and dancing shadows.

Jim was the first to speak.

"Whoa."

"Oh, *don't worry about me,*" Mickey chided.

"*I'll be fine!*" Beau mimicked.

"You fucking shot me," Jace moaned, cradling his arm. The same arm the—thing—had grabbed.

The flames died down, leaving only a greasy spot on blackened asphalt.

"How'd you even find me?" Jace asked.

"Had you on the drone soon as you left the bar," one of the newcomers said. "Cute kid like you, all alone, figured it couldn't resist." He softened somewhat. "Took us this long to catch up. Sorry."

"Oh,' Jace managed before passing out.

He woke to his worst nightmare (until now): flat on his back in a windowless van. Panic spiked as he reached for his blade.

"Easy, Jace, easy," Beau said. "They took it."

"They took everything," Mickey lamented, fingering his loose-fitting hospital scrubs with disdain. "Even our clothes."

"Had to," called a voice from behind the driver's compartment, behind the metal grate. "That thing's blood was all over them. The infirmary fixed you boys up pretty good, though. On the house."

"Yeah," Jim said. "Decontamination was a blast."

The van came to a stop, and the door slid open to reveal the XES lounge.

"Out," their rescuer said.

But he lingered with his hand on the door after they hobbled to the sidewalk. "Hey. None-a-my-business, of course, but you boys should maybe head south for a while. This thing last night, he ain't the only one."

"Unless you'd rather stay," drawled the driver as his companion climbed back in. "We could use some decent gator-bait."

With that, they sped off, and Jace lost sight of them in the morning traffic.

10

Mineshaft

TJ Tarbet

KLAXON. A sharp breath, and Sergeant Yales was upright, blankets off, reaching for a rifle that wasn't there. He palmed around in the dark, heart thudding against his ribcage. His phone wailed and danced on the nightstand, light leaking from the face down screen. Yales stared at it, stupefied. He shook his head.

That's right.

He grabbed it and turned it up. The light seared his eyes. *Unknown Caller.* The phone jiggled in his hand like some small mammal trying to escape. He blinked, then rubbed his eyes and thumbed the *Accept Call* button and held it to his ear.

"Yales."

"Sorry to wake you at this hour, Agent."

"No problem. I was already up."

A soft, feminine laugh. "Of course you were."

"Hey! I was!"

"Suuure."

"You calling me a liar?"

"Yes. And a shitty one, at that."

He snickered. "What's the situation?"

"We're not sure yet. We're calling it a mining accident. Very few eye-witnesses escaped, and those that did aren't really in a condition to talk. Amnesiacs have already been applied."

"You know I hate it when you guys do that."

Another laugh. "Really? You've only told me a dozen times now."

Yales rolled his eyes, sat down on the edge of his bed. "How bad is it?"

"A car will pick you up in fifteen minutes."

"Holy shit. What about my team?"

"Agents Willis and Carter are en route as we speak. Agent Schmidt is currently being contacted."

"What about Barnes?"

"He has yet to recover from the *last* mission you took him on."

"His leg wasn't that bad."

"PTSD, genius. I could list the anti-psychotics they have him on, but you don't have the time."

"Oh. That makes more sense."

"God. You are so dense some times."

He snorted, then grew quiet. "Is he gonna be okay?"

The line was silent.

"Jenny—"

"He's asked to be relieved. They're going to grant it when he can pass a psych eval."

Yales ran a hand down his face. He wasn't sure how to feel. On the one hand, Barnes was probably going to be all right, but on the other—

"This job isn't for everyone, you know," she said, gently.

"I know. I know. Does he blame me?"

"He's not really in a condition to blame anyone at the moment, Tiger."

Yales smirked. "Fair enough. Can you tell him—?"

"I'll do what I can."

"Thanks. I owe you."

"You bet your ass you do. I just broke, like, twenty rules for you."

"And I appreciate every one. So what about his replacement?"

"That's a negative. You're going in a man down this time."

"Just when I thought you cared—"

"It's out of my hands. All the agents in this sector are otherwise occupied. Hell, *you* weren't supposed to go active for another ten days."

"No big deal. I was getting bored anyway. Speaking of the mission, what about my briefing?"

"You and your team will be briefed. They're still putting the data together."

A low whistle. "That bad, huh?"

"You know I'm not supposed to speculate on missions."

"You do anyway."

"Fuck you."

"Any time, baby."

He could nearly hear Jenny's eyes roll. "Shouldn't you be packing?"

"It's called a go-bag, lovely. All I've got to do is throw on my pants, which means I've got all the time in the world to listen to your sexy, sexy—"

The line went dead.

"Jenny?"

———

The mine was nearly abandoned. A few cars peppered the gravel parking lot. He coasted among them, the gravel groaning under his tires like a man on his death bed. There it was. Big black SUV. They never skimped on those, he thought bitterly. Too bad he couldn't take it. He parked and dug around in his pocket for the other keys and hit the unlock button. The SUV's lights flashed. Yep. This was the one. Yales turned off the engine and hopped out of the car, shaking his head. Sure, the first-response teams got sweet rides, but the actual recon teams had to do with shitty rentals. The world was so unfair.

"Took you long enough."

Yales spun around. Agent Carter was leaning against the hood of another car. A grotesque pink bubble emerged from her lips, then popped, covering her nose. She pulled the gum back into her mouth with her tongue and chewed.

"That's nasty, Carter."

"You're just mad I'm better with my tongue than you are." She pulled her sunglasses down and winked. "So what's in the back?"

Yales shrugged. "The usual."

"Did you get Thor? Please tell me you got Thor."

"Yes, I got Thor."

Carter whooped and danced, running over to the back of the SUV with Yales, who was already pulling the doors open. A great black horizontal safe sat in the back, occupying the entirety of the passenger bay.

"Turn away, Carter."

"Aw, come on. It's not like everyone doesn't already know your stupid old code already."

"Turn away."

"Oh-seven-nine-eight-five-six."

Yales glared at her. "I'm not telling you again."

Carter frowned and shook her head, but turned away. Once Yales was sure she wasn't going to peek over her shoulder, he typed in the code.

079856

The top of the safe lifted and the end folded down. Carter was instantly at his elbow. "Where's my baby?" she squealed. "There he is!"

Yales had to jump back as Carter pushed her way between him and the car, heaving out a case that was a good foot taller than she was, hugging it and swinging it around like a long lost child, cackling the whole time.

"You aren't setting it up."

"What?!"

"You heard me. Grab your .338."

"But—"

"That's an order, Carter."

She pursed her lips but said nothing, setting the case down and stroking it before pulling out a much smaller one labeled *Loki*. Yales shook his head, pulling one of the P90s from the safe and sliding a mag home. Just as he was charging the weapon, another car rolled up and parked. It was tiny, bright green, the front bumper barely clearing the ground. The lights flicked off and the thing creaked and sank to one side. A huge black man with a donut in his mouth and a great pink box in his hands lurched out of the car. The car rose, groaning, as his weight lifted. His face was wide, the color of seared wood, and when he saw Yales he laughed around the donut, bit it, grabbed it in one hand and used it to point at Carter. "I told you we'd be back in time! He ain't even cracked open the gun case, has he?"

Yales cocked an eye brow and looked up from his weapon. "Good to see you too, Schmidt. You brought enough for every-one, or are you gonna eat all those yourself?"

Schmidt laughed again. "One dozen for me, another for the rest of you. Sue's got the coffee."

Yales leaned back, taking another look at the tiny green car they'd come in. "You mean you fit someone else in that clown car?"

The passenger door cracked open and a short, dark-haired woman stepped out, burdened with cups. She was pale, with a sharp nose and a sharper chin, hair cropped short, uneven. As if she might have cut it herself. "They didn't have one of those carrier things at the coffee shop, so come get yours before they burn me."

Yales replaced the weapon as Carter skipped behind him, grabbed a cup and a donut, then perched on the hood of the little green car.

"How come you're driving this tiny piece of shit, Schmidt?" Yales asked, relieving Willis of the second-to-last cup of coffee.

Schmidt shrugged. "It was what they had."

"And you didn't think to ask to trade with anyone?"

"Well, you see, Sue drove with me, and Carter—"

"I wouldn't take it." She smiled and winked at Schmidt. "I like driving *big* things."

Schmidt, to his credit, coughed and looked away. He might have been blushing. Yales wasn't sure. It was difficult to tell with how dark his skin was.

"Lay off the newbie, Carter." He took a bear claw from the box. At least Schmidt had good taste in donuts.

"So what's the situation, Yales?" Willis had a glazed donut in one hand and her coffee in the other. The donut had a bite out of it, but Willis didn't seem to be chewing.

"You know. Typical recon stuff. Shit for intel. Lots of dead people. High probability of a big scary monster. You know. Same shit, different day."

Carter giggled. Schmidt smiled and tried to laugh, but he couldn't seem to get it going. Like an old diesel on a cold morning.

Willis nodded, turned to the mouth of the mine. "I suspected as much."

Yales looked at the mine entrance. It seemed to gape, darker than it had any right to be. Of course, the sun was coming up over the mountain behind it, already caressing the valley below. That might account for some of it.

Some of it.

Yales walked up to Willis, stood beside her. "What do you see, Sue?"

She glanced at him, then back to the mine. Another bite of her donut was gone, but Yales hadn't seen her open her mouth except to speak. "It's old."

"They usually are."

"Indeed."

"Can you give me anything else?"

Willis stared at the mine.

Yales sighed, patted Willis on the shoulder, then turned back to Carter and Schmidt. Carter was halfway through a second donut, or perhaps a third. The girl could pack it away. She scooted closer to Schmidt, flipping her hair and giggling. Schmidt, almost twice her height, glanced at her, then at the pine trees, then back to her, then at the mine, then to her and away again.

"Carter!" Yales barked.

The donut flew from Carter's hand and a bit of coffee spilled onto her pants. She swore.

"If you're done flirting, go get set up."

With Carter, at least, it was easy to tell when she was blushing. She grabbed another donut, stuffed it in her mouth, then grabbed a napkin and scurried off like an embarrassed squirrel.

Yales leaned on the car. Carter had left a warm spot. Schmidt's eyes danced around the parking lot, and he grabbed another donut, then took a swig of his coffee only to find it gone. Yales offered him his own cup and Schmidt took it. The cup looked tiny in Schmidt's hands, as if it were a doll's cup. Yales looked up at him and smirked, then looked after Carter as she lugged a case towards the mine entrance.

"Cute, isn't she?"

Schmidt didn't answer.

"She's a handful, though. I've known her since I joined up. Pissed as hell when I got a squad and she didn't. We used to butt heads all the time." He laughed. "She's the best shot I've ever seen, though. Saved my life more than once."

A murmur. A sniff. Another slurp of coffee. From the tilt of the cup it looked mostly gone already.

"She doesn't like rules, though. It took me a while, but I've learned to overlook the less meaningful infractions. Keeps the team running smoother." He looked up at Schmidt again.

The man looked down at him, then to the mine. He kept his head shaved, and his eyes were a disturbing shade of blue. The shade of the polar sky. The kind of blue that killed.

Those eyes always looked out of place in Schmidt's friendly face.

Yales flung the other half of his donut across the gravel lot and into the trees. "Finish your coffee. I want to send one of your drones in there before we do anything serious."

Schmidt nodded and Yales stuck his thumb and then his pointer finger in his mouth, sucking off the glaze.

"Sir?"

Yales turned back. Schmidt's eyes were on the mine.

"Is it always this quiet?"

Yales glanced at the mine, then at the woods. No birdsong. No squirrel chatter. Even the trees seemed to be holding their breath.

"You get used to it. You stay in the field long enough and it starts to follow you. Animals mostly. Some people, if they're sensitive enough."

"That's—" Schmidt rubbed his arm. "That's creepy." He had a voice like a diesel engine, deep and smooth. Like what a submarine might sound like if it could talk.

"It ain't so bad. Keeps the bugs away." He laughed. "Haven't had a mosquito bite in years."

———

"What the hell is that thing on your face, Schmidt?"

Pearly teeth, like tombstones in the night, slid from behind Schmidt's lips as he slid the large, boxy thing from around his eyes up onto his forehead. "You like it? It's a VR setup. Made it myself." He picked up the quadcopter where it rested on its stand. It was nearly as long as Yales' arm, but it looked tiny and fragile in Schmidt's hands. "See the camera mount on the bottom? It'll track where I look, see?" He turned his head, slowly from side to side, and the little camera panned as well, servos whining like demonic crickets. "Did it all myself. You won't believe how long it took me to—"

"Yeah, yeah. I don't need a tech briefing. Just get the damn thing ready."

Schmidt's smile disappeared and he replaced the drone on the stand. "Yes, sir. Just finishing up some—I mean I just gotta synch the—"

Carter bumped Schmidt with her shoulder. "Don't worry

about Lieutenant Grumpy over there. He doesn't appreciate fine technical gadgetry." She had her tactical vest on over a sleeveless shirt. Emblazoned across it in blocky white embroidery was the phrase, SUN'S OUT, GUNS OUT.

"It won't matter. You won't get very far. He knows we're here." Willis stood leaning against the entrance to the mine, staring into the abyss. She used to blink. Yales swore she used to blink.

"Just get a screen set up so the rest of us can see."

"Yeah! Of course, sir. No problem."

The gravel crunched beneath Yales' feet like the bones of mice. He stopped next to Willis. "How bad is it?"

"Bad."

Hands on hips, staring down the nearly tangible dark. Behind him, the words, "Hold this for me?" "Oh, I'll hold anything you want, Bobby." Coughing. Shuffling.

"You gonna give me anything useful?"

"No." She did not look at him.

"Can you give me something, at least?"

One breath. Two. Three. "He's old. He was old when this planet was newborn. Bound. Angry. His chains are slipping."

Yales kicked at the gravel. The rocks jumped and skittered and fell silent. "Can we kill it?"

"You cannot kill that which can eternal lie."

"How did I know you were gonna say that?"

"Then why ask?"

He glanced back at Carter and Schmidt, then into the tunnel again. The light reached no more than five meters before the shadows claimed it. "Hope, I guess."

"We are not in the business of hope, Sam."

His heart tittered in his chest like a snare drum. Too much

coffee. "No, I suppose we aren't." He turned. "That drone ready to fly yet?"

"Yes sir."

Yales threw his thumb over his shoulder at the waiting dark. "Send it in."

Schmidt nodded. He lowered the visor over his eyes, then threw a series of switches on his controller. The rotors screamed like breathless cicada, kicking up dust, and the drone lifted off, tilted forward, and flew over Yales' head and into the dark.

Yales turned and watched the drone's light until it disappeared. "How far has it gone?"

"Forty, no, fifty meters."

"What kinda light you got on it?"

"A fifteen-hundred-lumen LED. I think something's wrong with the battery, though. It's not giving off the light it should be."

The snare drum in Yales' chest tittered faster. This wasn't going to be a pleasant mission. Were they ever, though? He turned and walked back to where the screen was set up.

It was a portable seven-inch LCD with wires that spider-webbed between a black box with an antenna and Schmidt's headset. Carter held the screen in her hands, then tilted it for Yales.

"Not much to see, boss."

Not much, indeed. Motes of dust in the dark. "You sure we're getting signal, Schmidt?"

"Yes, sir."

And yet nothing but motes of dust, like little floating teeth.

"Pan the camera around."

A grunt, and Schmidt's head craned slowly down. A white horizon rose from the bottom of the screen. Concrete. Inset rails. To the left. Ribs of concrete, like the segments of a gigantic caterpillar.

"Well, we're getting *something*, even if it is dark," Carter said.

Yales grunted, and bits of static started to flit lengthwise across the screen like little moths.

"What the hell is going on? Son of a—I'm only 300 meters out for Chrissakes." A huff. "I'm gonna try boosting the signal." He was talking more to himself than anyone else; already his hands were dancing across knobs on the controller, on the black antennaed box sitting next to him. The static tore the screen in spinning fragments, then receded again. "That's better."

"Keep her slow, Schmidt."

A murmur. The progress of the caterpillar ribs slowed, then slowed again. "How far in are we?"

"Three hundred twenty meters or so."

"Where was the service station supposed to be?"

"Uhhh—" Like the drowning of an overgrown bumblebee.

"About a hundred yards in," Carter piped in.

"Meters, Carter. Meters."

"I know what I said. Unlike *you*, *I* know that meters and yards aren't the same thing.

Yales shook his head, then glanced to Schmidt. "Why didn't we see it?"

Schmidt stared straight ahead with that black box on his face. It was like talking to a blind man.

"I don't know, sir. Light was probably too dim."

Yales grunted, then ran a hand over his mouth. He stared at the screen, then at the mine entrance, then at the screen again. "Spin it around."

"Sir?"

"Spin it around. Slow."

"Uh—okay."

The screen went from black to concrete caterpillar ribs to black again. Sweat pecked Schmidt's forehead. "What? We ain't *that* far in—musta gotten turned around somehow."

More caterpillar ribs. More black. More floating teeth dancing in the drone's flashlight. Schmidt's hands trembled.

"Uh—just a second, sir. Let me—"

"Don't worry about it. I kind of expected this. Try and get to the elevator if you can."

The visor slid up and onto Schmidt's forehead. Those eyes. Polar blue on white.

"Which way should I go?"

Yales cocked an eyebrow.

Schmidt swallowed, then nodded, mouth hanging open. He slid the visor down again, took a deep breath.

Silence but for breathing. The lights would flicker, fade, then come alive again, like a man struggling to stay awake. The screen would tear and fade, then the *tick tick* of Schmidt's controls would bring it back. Yales thought he could see faces in the static sometimes, and before long he could see faces in the darkness, too. Eyes and teeth. Never there when he looked right at them, but always hovering, playing in the eye's blind spots, flitting around the corners of the screen.

Before long, the static became too much and overwhelmed the screen completely. Schmidt flipped switches, spun knobs, but the image did not return. Schmidt lowered the antenna, peeled the visor away from his face, stared at the mine entrance. A sigh.

The drone had gone nearly a kilometer and never reached the elevator.

———

Yales stood before the yawning abyss. Vertigo nearly consumed him; it was like he was standing on a wall over a bottomless pit, deeper and darker than the reaches of space. Black—like that crazy new artificial black that absorbed like ninety-nine of all the light. Sucked up lasers like candy. *That* was a trip to look at. They'd made some suits out of it for some spec ops teams, only to find it made them stand out more. The operatives were blacker than the shadows they were hiding in. Scared the piss out of the people who saw them, though.

That stuff had nothing on this abyss.

He took a deep breath, one of many. They'd been standing here for nearly a minute, waiting for his go ahead. The command to plunge. No one talked. Nothing moved. No sound but for the whispering black in front of them. Nobody else wanted to take the dive, either.

The safety of his weapon ticked under his thumb. On-off-on-off-on-off-on-off. Felt rather than heard. *Go through the checklist again. That'll calm your nerves.*

no it wont

Armored vests? Check.

they wont do you any good

Lamps? Shoulder mounted, weapon mounted, head mounted. Check.

the black will eat your lights like it will eat your souls

Masks and filters? Check.

you cannot filter out the darkness

Fire support? He glanced over at Carter, splayed out on the ground, cheek resting on Loki's stock. Three screens set arm's length from her face. Camera feeds from their vests.

If there was something that had never failed him on a mission, it was Carter. He didn't know how much she'd do out here, but he wanted the cover if they had to make a hasty retreat.

Tech support? Schmidt already had his mask on, was tinkering with something under one of the lenses. Some sort of augmented reality bullshit.

newbies are always the first to go

Willis? Where did she even fit in? She refused to take anything more than a pistol on missions. She was good with it, so he'd learned not to argue. Her stare worried him, though. Had for a long time. What did she see in the dark?

she sees what waits in the dark

Well, they weren't getting any readier. He swallowed again. What were they forgetting? It was like camping. You always forgot something. He patted his spare mags. Five of them. Two hundred and fifty rounds. Another one already loaded. Ration bars. Water. This was supposed to be a short recon, but he didn't want to take any chances with what had happened to that drone. Glow sticks? Everyone had fifty. If they would work any better than their flashlights was anyone's guess.

Time to take the plunge. Past time. He loosened his jaw, sniffed. "Alright, enough waiting around. Masks on." He reached up and pulled his gas mask down over his face. One of the more reliable pieces of equipment they had. Supernatural or not, not a lot got through the air filters.

If they did, chances were you were dead, anyway.

"Comm check."

"Roger." Schmidt's voice rumbled in his earpiece at the same time he heard his muffled reply.

"Loud and clear, boss." Carter.

"I await the embrace of the dark."

"Goddamnit, Willis, why you gotta be like that?"

She looked at Yales. He could have sworn that he saw the hint of a smile behind the eyepieces. He shook his head.

"All right, boys and girls. Let's do this. Leeeroy Jenkins."

He charged his rifle and marched into the mine. The gravel crunched under his boots like cockroaches underfoot, then solid concrete. Why did they have a gravel parking lot? Who had gravel parking lots anymore?

The patter of their boots echoed in the mine proper. Spotlights dotted the walls, perhaps dimmer than they should have been. Another dozen paces in, Yales turned back. "Carter, you still read us?"

"Yeah, boss."

"The video coming through?"

"Better than ever. Bobby-boy's a miracle worker."

"I'm sure. Just keep your eyes off his ass while we're in here."

"That's gonna be awfully hard, boss. This scope's *really* good—"

"Yeah, yeah. Schmidt, get your camera rolling."

"Yes, sir." A click, barely heard. "This is Agent Schmidt on assignment 701-223. We are in Utah, the high Uintas, investigating a mine which has recently come under the influence of an unknown entity. I am accompanied by Agents Yales and Willis, and Agent Carter is covering the mouth of the mine. Preliminary scouting via drone has revealed very little."

They marched on, lights dancing on the floors, ceiling, and walls while Schmidt's voice hummed. Not only was Schmidt the newbie, but Yales liked his voice. At times, that deep bass rumble was their only tether back to normalcy.

Yales looked back at the entrance. It was smaller than, perhaps, it should have been; the size of his outstretched thumb. He held up a fist and the other two stopped. He looked back down into the mine. The dark swallowed the light from his headlamp. He felt like some fish at the bottom of the sea with a bioluminescent lure. A bit of light to attract smaller fish. Of course, the biggest fish didn't use lures. They ate the ones that did. He looked back at the entrance. Had it gotten smaller? The size of the tip of his index finger, now.

"Willis, start dropping breadcrumbs. Every ten meters."

No response but a sharp crack and a daub of phosphorescent green in the dark. She shook it and it grew, then she dropped it to the ground. It looked very small. Hopefully, it would be enough to lead them back.

"Alright, move out. Keep an eye out for the service station. I want to see if we can't turn on some lights."

"That won't work, Sam."

"Won't hurt to try, Sue."

Willis murmured, but Yales didn't catch it. He shook his head and moved on. At a hundred yards, they found the service station. A checkpoint, really. Candy cane barrier across the way, a little guard post. Inside, a door set into the rock face.

"Sue."

Willis nodded, advanced on the post. She didn't bother opening it, simply raised her boot and heeled in the door at the handle. The door cracked and stove in. The noise echoed in the dark, distorted to a deep laugh, then faded. Willis gave Yales a meaningful look, then strode into the box, light dancing along the walls, under the consoles, on the ceiling.

"Clear."

"Lights?"

"Won't do us any good."

"Just answer me."

Her light glided across the panel, then stopped. "They're already on."

"Toggle them."

Yales could hear Willis's eyes roll in the dark, but she said nothing. Click one two three four click. No sound but a shadow's breathing.

"Again."

Click one two three click then a deep crack and a double string of parallel lights burst to life along the ceiling, then another, then another on down the tunnel. What might have been a screech echoed in behind the sound of the deep whack of the lights advancing. Some flickered, but they did not falter. Yales nodded and Willis emerged from the booth, pupils shrinking. Still she didn't blink, even as Yales' and Schmidt's eyes fluttered like dying butterflies.

"Goddamnit, boss! Warn me next time," Carter crackled over the radio.

"Sorry." He turned to Willis. "Keep dropping breadcrumbs."

She nodded.

Yales took a deep breath. The mine curved downward and to the right in another fifty meters. That might have been why Schmidt hadn't been able to find the elevator. Might have been.

"Keep your lights and masks on and your eyes open. Those lights probably won't last long. We find the worker access elevator and send one of Schmidt's drones down. If we determine it to be safe, we'll keep going. If not, we back out. Let's go."

As they went, Yales got more and more tense. Those lights were entirely too large for a mine of this size. They were like stadium lights, baking the inside of the mine with a blank white. Mines didn't use lights like this, didn't need them, didn't want the expense of installation or of maintenance. At least, he thought they didn't. All his expertise came from movies, but it still felt wrong.

They reached the elevator in silence. Not so much an elevator as a lift; an open shaft behind a diamond-grate barrier, cables and pulleys and the gaping abyss crawling up the braided steel and the rock walls. Yales hammered the lift button with the heel of his hand, then put his back to the wall, pointed the muzzle of his submachine gun at the crisscrossing steel. Willis mirrored him on the opposite side, and Schmidt knelt before the diamond mesh as if to be knighted, weapon at his shoulder. Motors whirred somewhere above them, and the cables blurred. Time passed in heartbeats, and finally the empty lift appeared.

"How much cable do you have?"

"Two hundred meters."

Yales grunted, and Schmidt clicked on the safety and let his weapon hang from his harness and set his pack on the ground. He pulled out an RC car and a spool of cable. He made to put his visor on again, but Yales clicked his tongue. Schmidt looked up.

"Use a screen."

Schmidt opened his mouth, then looked down the curving tunnel, and back to the lift, and nodded. "We sending it down the lift or the ramp, sir?"

"Lift."

Schmidt nodded, plugged a touchpad in to the spool of wire and the screen winked to life. He tapped the screen several times, then put his thumbs on the virtual joysticks and the camera on top of the little machine panned back and forth, the front wheels jerked left and right, and then the car screeched back, then forward. Schmidt nodded to Yales. "Everything's optimum, sir."

Yales nodded and lifted the gate for the drone. It screamed on to the lift like a brat or a banshee, and then spun around. Yales closed the gate.

"Wait, is the cable gonna get pinched on the way down?"

"We're about to find out." Yales heeled the down button and the lift sank and the cables spooled down the shaft.

Nothing caught, and Schmidt heaved a sigh.

"The Institute pays for stuff like that, you know."

"Doesn't mean it ain't a lot of work to fix."

Yales shrugged. "Willis, keep an eye on the shaft. I want to know if anything bigger than a cockroach crawls up it. Schmidt, you do your thing." He turned to the ramp and went to one knee. "I'll watch this way."

Murmurs of affirmation, then silence. Almost silence. The sound of motors whirring and cable spooling and the lights above him flickered and buzzed and hummed. He glanced up. They seared his eyes, but they looked to be LEDs. They shouldn't be making any noise at all. He sniffed, then settled his weapon to his shoulder and watched the ramp.

A sudden clank and Yales jumped. "We've reached the first level, sir."

"What do you see?"

"Well, the safety barrier's already up. Lights are on down there too."

Yales glanced at Willis. She cocked an eyebrow. Yales swallowed and nodded. Yales took a deep breath and looked back down the shaft. Yales tightened his grip on his weapon.

"What else?"

"Not much. Everything seems clear. No movement. No audio. Nothing that shouldn't be there."

Yales forced his jaw to unclench. "Proceed." The thumping of his heart was nearly louder than the sound of his voice.

"Roger." Schmidt's great black thumbs slid against the screen and the cable began to unspool again.

"Left clear. Right—clear. Proceeding right. There's a big orange truck. Looks like a dump truck. It's empty. There's an

intersection up ahead. Clear on the right. Clear on the
—whoa."

"Whoa?"

"The lights at the end just went out. There goes another
one." Schmidt tilted his head to one side. "It's like they're failing
one after another."

"Shit. Pull your—" Then came the sound of a muffled bell
from the shaft, then again and again, louder with each keen,
and then the lift cable snapped with a screech and an echoing
peal. Schmidt's cable whirred out of the spool, then was gone,
pulling the controller right out of Schmidt's hands and down
the shaft. Schmidt stared after it, mouth agape.

"Son of a—what just—"

A crash echoed through the tunnel, and dust vomited out of
the lift shaft and covered them. As the sound faded, another
sound came from down the ramp, a great crack, and then
another, and another. Closer and closer.

"Move."

Willis was off like a gazelle. Yales followed her at half a
dozen paces, then looked back. Schmidt was gathering up his
equipment and stuffing it into his bag. Yales pounced on him
and pulled him to his feet. "Leave it!"

Another crack, and one of the lights on the ramp went out,
then another. Yales spun Schmidt to the entrance and pushed
him, heart pounding at his sternum.

Too late. If you had to run, it was already too late.

They ran anyway.

The lights failed faster and faster, flashing and thundering
like lightning, then gone. Glass showered Yales and Schmidt,
then the lights in front of him failed in quick succession, a
string of fireworks up to the entrance. Dark swallowed them
like a cold fog.

Much too late.

"Halt!" Yales and the other two skidded to a stop. Training over instinct. Running into something they didn't see in the dark was a lot more dangerous at this point than whatever might be chasing them.

"Back to back. Willis, you're our eyes. Follow the glo sticks. Move."

Yales' heart beat in his throat, his ears, as if it had been duplicated and transposed. As if these new locations were somehow better for his survival than his chest. He pressed his back to the backs of the other two, forming a three-pointed star, weapon hard against his shoulder, light from shoulder and weapon mounted flashlights dancing on the floor, the ceiling, the wall. Schmidt, tall, solid, hot, on his right. Willis on his left. Small. Cold. He wasn't even sure she was breathing hard.

"You got eyes on our breadcrumbs, Willis?"

"Most of them, yeah."

"Can you see the entrance?"

"Not yet. Breadcrumbs haven't failed us yet, though."

Yales took a deep breath, forced his weapon to stop shaking. He pushed two fingers against his ear. "Carter, you read? Carter!"

Nothing. Not even static. Everlasting fuck.

"Alright, people. We've done this before. Willis, pop a flare and lead us out. Schmidt, you see anything moving, anything, you fill it full of lead. Stay in formation. Move."

A pop and a hiss and then red, like a bleeding piece of the sun, illuminated the tunnel. Shadows leered on the walls of the tunnel, parodies of faces, claws that disappeared under the white glare of his weapon light. Should have brought a laser. Things like this always hated lasers. Yales didn't know why. Didn't care. He hated the way they could attract attention, give away his position, but he swore for the hundredth time that if they got out of this, he'd start mounting laser sights on every single one of his weapons.

If they got out.

Where the tunnel had seemed to echo at every opportunity before, the dark now seemed to swallow every sound they made. Yales could hear little more than his own breathing, hot and loud inside his mask. Even the patter of his boots seemed small and far away, as if his feet and legs had been excised and given to someone else, and he were merely floating along the dark. He could feel Willis and Schmidt's shoulders as they moved down the tunnel, as they each readjusted their aim.

"How we doing, Sue?"

"Flare's dying."

"What? It's been two minutes!"

"Look."

Yales chanced a glance. The flare was already burning low. A moment later it began to sputter.

"Son of a whore's ass."

"You shouldn't try to be creative with your curses, Sam. You're not good at it."

"We're about to be eaten by a shadow monster, and you're giving me grief about how I swear?"

Willis shrugged against him, and a moment later the flare popped and fizzled and died, and the flashlights on the ends of their weapons began to flicker. Yales' lungs shrank and his heart began to beat against his ribcage as if it might burst forth and run on its own. He swallowed.

"We—" Scmidt began. "We ain't really gonna get eaten, are we, sir? Cause I don't wanna be—I mean, I never figured—"

Their flashlights died.

"Fucking shitballs." Yales hit the light with the heel of his hand. "Tell me you've got another flare, Sue."

"Too late."

"What do you mean, 'Too late?' Cut the mystic crap and just give me a straight answer for once in your goddamned—"

The darkness laughed and Yales' flashlight sputtered to life, revealing a great yellow eye lidded with teeth.

Yales fired.

The eye burst like a pustule, showering him in cold, black muck.

"Run!" He held down the trigger, emptying the entire magazine, running as he reloaded, then dumping that one into the darkness as well. The muzzle flashes from their weapons revealed a wall of eyes and teeth and tentacles, all laughing, all screeching. One tentacle reached out and grabbed Willis by the ankle and she went down hard. Yales skidded to a halt and grabbed her by the vest. He fired at the thing until it came apart, then yanked her to her feet.

"Carter! Carter, if you can hear this we're gonna need some cover fire!"

Static.

"Carter!"

More static.

He tore out another magazine and slapped it into place. Last one. If they didn't get out of here soon—

Something whizzed past his head and a heartbeat later a crack that echoed and left his ears ringing. The dark howled and recoiled for a moment, and then another round impacted and it howled again.

Thank God for Carter!

A roar shook the mountainside, reverberating through his bones, nearly shook him to the ground. Schmidt stumbled, nearly fell, but kept running, kept firing. A moment later he cried, "I'm out!"

"Just run!" Yales dumped the last of his rounds as well, and the darkness roared again and lashed out, full of writhing tentacles and teeth. Another round from Carter, but this time the darkness did not recoil, closing in on him and Willis and Schmidt.

"Carter, tell me you've got Thor set up."

Through the radio in a haze of snow and static, Yales heard, "I thought you'd never ask."

A heartbeat. Two. Three. Too long. Yales could feel the dark reaching out, cold breath on his neck, teeth on his ears, whispers in his bones. *Insolent insects,* they said. *I will rend your flesh and your souls. I will swallow you whole in the name of my eternal hunger. I will—*

What felt like a freight train whizzed past and impacted with an echoing slap. The dark howled in rage and pain and a report shattered the air.

"Good job, Carter!"

"It's a little soon to say I told you so, but—"

"Just keep firing!"

Another round echoed in the tunnel. They were going to go deaf before long, but Yales didn't really care. His hair shuffled in the breeze of another round and another wet slap echoed in the tunnel, follow by the deafening blast of Carter's weapon. He could see the entrance, and he pushed himself harder. Fifty meters. They were going to make it.

"Reloading."

Or maybe not. He'd forgotten that Thor only held three rounds.

He'd been counting on five.

He ran. Among the howls of the creature behind them, he

could hear the patter and the breathing of Schmidt and Willis. Come on, keep running. A rush of air, and something passed over his head and he ducked out of instinct. Thirty meters. A screech that shook the tunnel and Yales stumbled. Eighteen meters. Dark closed in on the edge of his vision and he couldn't tell if it was his mask fogging or a lack of oxygen or if the thing itself was closing in. Ten meters. He could feel the creature's breath dewing on the back of his arms, the back of his neck, could feel it tickling the back of his mind.

You are mine. I shall thieve you away, show you such beautiful pain, such wonderful—

Carter fired again and the muzzle blast hit Yales like an ocean wave, and he stumbled, almost fell. The darkness screeched behind him and he and Schmidt and Willis burst out into the blinding sunlight, heaving and gasping. Yales tore the mask from his face and his weapon harness from his torso, then tore at the straps to his ballistic vest and threw it on the ground along with his shirt. The discarded clothes steamed in the sunlight, and his skin was cold and white where the creature's ichor had seeped through the fabric. He touched it and winced, and his fingertips came away white as well. White and steaming.

"Saline," he snapped. Willis was already in motion, ripping open a medpack and rushing over to him with a liter bottle of emergency eyewash as he tore off his shoes, pants, and boxers. The white had spread below his waist, but no lower. Small blessings.

Particularly small, in this case. Fear did not have a flattering effect on one's privates. Willis handed him the bottle and he twisted the cap off and drenched himself, the slime coagulating and running off his flesh like fleeing leeches.

"Wooo!" Carter was laughing. "Didya see that? It was like

the whole goddamned mine came alive. It was all, 'Wraaaa!' and 'Skeeee!'" She mimed with her hands and mouth, sounding for the life of her like a dying tyrannosaurs rex. She reached down and picked up her 20mm rifle, a weapon that was taller than she was, and rested the butt on her cocked hip, then immediately lost her balance and fell onto her ass.

Yales fell to his knees, gasping, and looked back, saline solution dripping from his face and chest. There were a hundred teeth glistening there and twice as many eyes glinting, all swimming around in random drifts and eddies, disappearing and opening and closing and smiling at him.

This is not the end, they said. *You will return. And even if you do not, I will come for you. I will find you. This paltry prison cannot hold me for much longer.*

"Sue," Yales heaved. "Sue, what the hell was that?"

Willis was on her back, staring at the sky. She merely shook her head.

Schmidt groaned and stumbled to the munitions van and leaned against it. "Is it always like this with you guys?"

Yales gave half a laugh then started to cough. He sniffed, swallowed, his throat dry and cracking. "Yeah. What did you expect?"

"I don't know. Bigfoot, or something."

Yales fell back onto the gravel and laughed hysterically.

11

Wishing You Weren't Here
Maxwell Alexander Drake

It's easy to pick out the crazy people in a crowd.
They're the ones acting differently from the rest of us.
However, should that really be the definition of crazy?

What if it's us who are crazy,
and only a few unlucky individuals
are able to see life as it really is?

MAD

YOU REACH out to the tape recorder sitting on the table before you, then pause. All your searching, all your sacrifice, and now you finally have what you've been looking for. Answers. Answers to how all this happened. Answers to what caused the end of humanity.

Letting your finger caress the *PLAY* button for a second, you press it down. A crackling pop stabs your ears as the machine bursts to life. The gears of the cassette turn for the first time in decades, and the squeaks of plastic rubbing plastic fill the dark room you have found refuge in.

An old man's voice, rough and dry, reverberates through the speakers. "So, am I just supposed to start talking?"

The loud screech of metal scraping across a concrete floor forces you to turn the volume down. You glance at the door to the room. Even as thick as it is, you know it won't protect you for long. But you must know, even if it costs you your life. You turn your attention back to the tape player as a younger man's voice spills from it.

"Just give me a moment please, James, and we will begin." The man clears his throat. "This is Doctor Simon Reynolds speaking, doctor of pathology here at the Nevada Mental Health Institute in Sparks, Nevada. The time is eight thirty-two in the a.m. on Monday, November thirteenth, 1989. I am here with patient James Martin, who has been a resident of this institution since 1949. We are in conference room three."

The doctor pauses a moment and takes a deep breath before continuing. His voice is softer now. More kind. "How are you today, James?"

"Um, fine, I s'pose."

"Good, good. James, I've been asked by the State to have a chat with you. Do you know why?"

"Not really, no." The man named James coughs.

"Well," the doctor says, "you are up for parole next month and—"

"No, no, no, no," James says. You imagine him shaking his head as he repeats the word.

"I'm sorry. Does this news upset you, James?"

"Don't want no parole."

There is a pause.

"But, James. Don't you want to be free of this hospital? You have been here for a long time."

Another pause.

"Don't you want to experience what life is like outside these walls?"

The tape recorder crackles for a few seconds, relaying the uncomfortable silence from years past.

The doctor prompts, "James?"

Reluctantly, the old man answers. "I just—"

"You just what, James?"

"It ain't safe out there!"

"Why do you think it isn't safe, James?"

"You have my file. You know why, same as all the others who read it."

"Do you still think it was *zombies* that day, James?" The sound of doubt coats the doctor's tone.

"If not zombies, then monsters for true. I saw what I saw!" James says, his voice rising to a loud croak.

"I'm not saying you didn't, James. Please, there is no reason for raised voices." For a moment, bodies shifting in chairs are the only sounds that emanate from the recorder. "Do you feel we can continue?"

"Yeah. I guess so." The older man sounds calm once more.

"Good, good. I have read the case file from the—*incident*— back in forty-nine."

"And?"

"And what, James?"

"Does it say I'm crazy?"

"It says many things, James. But there is much it does not say, as well."

"Like what?" James asks, his tone snide.

"Like whether or not you're crazy."

Both men fall silent. In your mind's eye, you picture them in a cold, desolate room—two men: one old, one young—sitting in metal chairs staring at each other across a metal table. White walls surround them, interrupted only by a metal door, and a tiny window with bars. You wonder what it would be like to live for forty years in such a place.

"May I ask you a question, James?"

"That's why we're here, ain't it?"

"Do *you* think you're crazy?"

"No."

"You answered that quickly." The doctor sounds amused.

"It's been forty years, Doc. Don't need no more time to think on that."

A shuffling of papers crackles over the recording.

"Have you thought about that night?"

The pop and hiss of the aged cassette rolls on alone for nearly a minute without either man speaking. Finally, the doctor breaks the silence.

"We don't have to talk about this if you don't want to, James."

"No." The old man sounds timid, afraid. Yet, his voice holds a hint of intent as well. "I—I think I need to tell my side. At least once."

"I've read your statement, James. The one you made right after the police arrested you."

"I doubt they wrote everything I said. *They* sure thought I was crazy. Besides, they saw me as guilty as soon as they found me."

"Do you blame them?"

"Not no more. Still, they didn't really ask me no questions."

"The report *is* rather sparse of details. I would very much like to hear your story, James. If you feel like telling it."

The old man did not answer verbally, though there is a sigh and the rustling of movement.

"Good, good. Why don't you start from the beginning, James? Take me back to that night."

The old man doesn't respond.

"You were staying at the San Souci Court on the day of the incident, correct? I found this old postcard when I was doing research on your case. I thought it might help you remember things. It has a picture of what the hotel looked like back then, see?"

The sound of someone flicking thick paper comes across the speakers.

"You know," says the doctor, "the San Souci is gone now. They demolished it a few years ago, right after Steve Wynn purchased the land. The Mirage sits there now. A beautiful building. They say it's a hotel to 'usher in a new era' for the Vegas Strip. After seeing it, I'm a believer. It's massive, James. Unlike anything there now. I think it opens in a few weeks."

"I don't care 'bout none of that." James does not sound amused.

"Of course not. Still, that's what's there now. Things change, James. The world moves forever forward. What was it like all those years ago?" the doctor asks.

"It was nice enough, even back then." A chair creaks. "You much of a gambling man, Doc?"

"Not really. I go down to the strip from time to time for one thing or another. But I wouldn't call myself a gambling man, no."

"Well, I was. Back in the day." The old man sounds wistful

now. "There was just something about the turn of a card that got my pulse a-racin'."

"You liked cards, then?"

"Oh, you bet, Doc. And I was darn good, too. Lady Luck was kind to me. And when she wasn't, I could bluff a man right out of his shoes, I could. Make him doubt his own mama."

"Is that what you were playing the night of the incident, James?"

"Yeah. I was sittin' at a table with four others. Weren't none of us talking, though. Cards were turning, chips were changing hands. Never asked any of 'em their names."

"Were there others in the room?" the doctor asks.

"A few. Sam, the bartender, was doing his thing. A couple girls serving the tables. But, other than our dealer, that was all. But you already know how many people were in the room, don't ya, Doc?"

Again, papers shuffle. "The police report says there were ten people in that room other than yourself. But that doesn't mean I know how many were there before—" The doctor trails off. You get the sense that he's uncomfortable.

"Before I killed them, you were gonna say."

"That is *not* what I was going to say, James. Other people could have been in that room. People who left before the incident."

"No. Not one person who was there ever left that room again—ceptin' me."

"What happened, James?"

You listen as the tape turns, the occasional pop or hiss filling the emptiness. Finally, the old man named James takes a deep breath and lets it out slowly. "It all started when Ted burst into the room. Ted was the handyman. I had seen him around, said a kind word in passing. Didn't know him beyond that." The tone in the man's voice takes on an edge of fear. "Ted was in a bad way. A real bad way. Covered in blood. His side, mostly. There was a large rip in his shirt just under his left arm. He was screamin' about something in the basement."

"Did he say what happened to him?" the doctor asks.

"No. It was all folks could do to calm him down. I stayed at the table, minding my own. At that point, I wasn't interested in how some fool had hurt himself."

"So you weren't concerned or curious?"

"A little. But I wanted the game to continue. If memory serves, I had aces over fours. Weren't no one going to beat me that round. Sam brought over some towels from the bar while the girls sat Ted down in a chair. They begun tendin' the wound on his side. Once the manager came in and looked at things, he told us everything was under control and we should just get back to our fun."

"And did you?"

"For a while. There was still a lot of fuss over Ted."

"Why didn't they move him to another room?"

"They tried. But, once they had him sat down, he just wouldn't be bothered with the moving. So they tended him there in the gambling hall."

"What happened then, James?" You feel like the doctor knows more than he's saying.

"We were playing another hand. I only had a pair of tens, but I was betting hard on 'em. Like I said, I could make a man doubt he was ever born. Chips had started building a nice pile in the center of the table since none of us had folded yet." James stops talking. The rhythmic sound of a chair rocking back and forth comes from the small speaker on the recorder.

"If this is upsetting you, James, we can stop," the doctor says in a comforting voice.

"No. No, I—I want ta' tell it."

"All right then. The pot was large. Did you win or lose?"

"We didn't finish that hand."

"Why not?"

"Because Sally screamed."

"And Sally was—?"

"One of the waitresses tending Ted. We all turned when she screamed, and we saw that Ted had fallen out of his chair. I didn't think nothin' of it until she yelled about him being dead."

"So, Ted—" The sound of papers shuffling spill from the recording again. "That would be Ted Mackenzie?"

"If you say so."

"He is listed here as the maintenance man for the casino. I'm asking if this is the same man."

"Yeah, Ted. The guy who cleaned up around the joint. Why are you grilling me about him, Doc?"

"I just want to make sure I understand the situation as you describe it. So, you are saying that Ted Mackenzie died in the gambling hall from a large wound in his side."

"Yeah. They even brought in a sheet to cover him with."

"And you are certain of this?"

"There's not much about that night I'm not, Doc. I've had plenty of time to think on it."

"Then how is it that Ted's body was found later with his head bashed in by a hammer?"

"Because Ted didn't stay dead."

The tape clicks to a stop. You fumble with the eject button. Something bangs in the hallway outside your room. You don't know how much time you have left, but you must find out what started all this, even if it's the last thing you do. With trembling fingers, you turn the tape over and slip it back into the machine. You close it and press *PLAY* once more.

"I'm sorry for the interruption." Frustration laces the doctor's words. "Please, let's continue. You were saying that Ted came back to life. But is there a chance Sally had been wrong about him being dead in the first place? Perhaps Ted had just passed out from blood loss."

"That'd be nice if it was true."

"So, you are certain."

"Look, Doc. That wasn't the first time I'd seen a dead body. He'd stopped bleeding, wasn't breathing. His eyes—they stared up at the ceiling all vacant like. The man was dead."

"Very well, James. Help me understand the events that happened after Sally screamed."

"Like I said, they brought in a sheet and covered him. The manager tried to get everyone to return to the game, but none of us really wanted to. We gathered around the bar, on the far side away from Ted's body. Sam poured out hefty shots of whisky for everyone at the manager's request."

"Something you said earlier brings up a question. You said no one left. With all that had just happened, I mean, a man died in that room, you would think that some would have wanted to leave."

"Oh, several wanted to split—me included."

"Why didn't you, James?"

"The manager wouldn't let us. He locked the damn doors, saying, 'The cops will want to ask ya'll questions.' Plus he gave us free whisky. Wasn't turning that down. So, everyone gathered around Sam as he poured us drinks."

"So, the five of you who were playing poker were now at the bar, drinking. How many drinks did you have?"

James laughs. "Yeah. The cops accused me of being drunk, too."

"Were you?"

"No. Before I even finished that first drink, Ted sat up."

"Just like that?"

"Pretty much. I was looking at him. Laying there under that sheet. Thinking what a waste it was to die working as a handy-man. Then the sheet slid off him as he sat up."

"Did anyone else notice?" the doctor asks.

"Not at first. I just sat there, my drink half way to my lips, looking right into his eyes."

"His vacant eyes?"

"Oh, no. Not this time, Doc. This time they were far from vacant. They were cold, burning with hate. Like he was angry at me for still being alive."

"Who noticed him next?"

"Sam said something first. Then Sally screamed again when she saw him sitting there. The other girl, I don't think I ever knew her name, knelt down next to him. She tried to ask him if he was okay. That's when he—it—grabbed her and bit into her neck. Just ripped right into her flesh with his teeth. I never seen so much blood pour outta one person." James stops again and a long silence fills the recording.

"Did anyone try and help the girl?" the doctor finally asks.

"We did. All of us. Me and Sam grabbed the girl, tried to pull her away. A bunch of the others went after Ted. Or what-ever he had become. I think that's when one of them got bit on the arm.

"The girl died in my arms, Doc." James' voice quivers as he continues. "Just gurgled a bit on the blood in her mouth. She looked terrified as she stared up at me. Her eyes begging me to do something. To make her—not die. Then she was gone."

"How did that make you feel, James?"

"I didn't feel nothing, Doc. I was —numb. My mind was still struggling with what was happening. I just laid her down between me and Sam. Then we went to help the others with Ted."

"They were not able to restrain him?" The doctor sounds genuinely shocked. "There were what, four or five men on him?"

"At first, I thought they had him. As I said, one of the guys got bit on the arm, but he was still in the fray. As me and Sam got near, Ted flung one of the men off. Practically threw him across the room.

"Sam slammed into Ted's chest, so I went for his legs. I'm telling you, Doc, even with all of us on him, we were making no headway. He was like a maniac. We even started hitting him, but it was as if he felt nothing.

"At some point in the struggle, he threw all of us off. I ended up behind the bar, stars filling my eyes after slamming my head on the back counter. When I came up, Ted was on top of one of the men, biting him in the face. The man was screaming even while Ted ripped his nose off. That's when I saw the hammer laying on the shelf behind the bar."

"And you used it on Ted Mackenzie."

"I had no choice!" James yells. "It wasn't Ted no more. That thing just knelt there, ripping bits of the guy's face off with his teeth. Everyone else just stood on, watching. I think they was all in shock. But I couldn't just stand by. The guy was still alive, still screaming, even while being eaten. So, yeah. I went up behind Ted and bashed him in the head with the hammer!"

"How many times did you hit Ted, James?"

"I don't know. Until he stopped moving."

"But Ted was not the only one you hit with the hammer. Was he, James?"

"No. It all happened so fast, I'm not sure how it all went down. I've tried to recreate the events in my mind, but it's all a blur. I know the girl with her throat ripped out came back to life next. She attacked Sam from behind. I don't remember the guy who had been bitten on the arm actually dying, but he also went into a frenzy and started attacking people at some point. I tried to get the girl off Sam, but it was too late. She had already sunk her teeth into his back. I remember hitting her with the hammer, though."

The tape rolls on without either man speaking.

Finally, the doctor's voice breaks the silence. "The report says when the cops found you, you were huddled behind the bar covered in blood, still clutching the hammer."

"Yeah. That sounds about right."

"It also says every single person in that room had their heads bashed in. That you were covered in blood from each of them."

"It does make me kinda look like the bad guy, don't it, Doc?"

Several seconds of tape run before the sounds of a chair creaking fills the void.

"I want to thank you for your time today, James."

"What about that parole? I still don't want it."

"Don't worry, James. I'm going to recommend to the State that they let you stay here at the hospital."

"Thanks, Doc."

"No problem, James."

There was a scraping of chair legs on concrete floor and the distinct sound of papers being gathered.

"Doc?"

"Yes, James?"

"I know you think I'm crazy, even though you didn't say it outright."

"James, it's not my job—"

"Let me finish, Doc. I just want to say, as far as I know, no one ever did figure out what attacked Ted and started that whole mess to begin with. Whatever he found in that basement —it's still there. There may be a shiny new casino sittin' on it now, but that don't mean that somewhere underneath, down in a sub-basement maybe, that there ain't some *thing* still down there. Waitin'.'"

"I'm sure everything will be fine, James. Everything will be just fine."

The tape recorder clicks off, leaving a heavy weight resting on your chest. Walking to the window, you pull back the curtains. The Vegas Strip stretches off to your left and right. Across the street, the Venetian stands tall and proud, its delicate stonework and balconies almost glow white in the moonlight. A few buildings away sits the Flamingo. Its crown, usually a burst of reds, pinks, and oranges, is dark. Glancing further to your right you see the top of the Eiffel tower of the Paris Casino. For your whole life, this city has been alive. Now, for the first time that you know of, it sits dark.

Well, you think to yourself, *the crazy old kook was right about one thing. Whatever attacked Ted Mackenzie was still down there.*

You just wish you had more time to find out what it was.

Letting your gaze drop to the street two stories below, you are greeted by a sea of bodies clogging every open space. Two to three million tourists shuffle about. If you did not know better, you would think it was just a normal night on the strip. However, when you look closer, you notice the oddities. A tall man with his jaw ripped off. A fat woman missing one arm. A fatal wound on each and every one of them, though none of them seemed to realize they should be dead and not walking around. Whenever one looks up and sees you, its cold eyes burn with hate.

You pull out your revolver and check the cylinder. Only one bullet left.

The pounding on your hotel room door resumes. The dead can smell you, and you know they will not rest until they get inside.

Letting out a heavy sigh, you place the gun to your temple, its barrel cold against your skin.

The door to the hotel room gives way and a pile of undead pour into the room. You lock eyes with the one in the lead. A blond woman with most of her side missing. Lengths of intestine dangle down her leg. She stares at you for what feels like an eternity, then lets out the wordless gurgle of a cry.

Just before you pull the trigger, you laugh at a thought that crosses your mind. *If the last person dies in a world full of zombies, does anybody really give a crap?*

You don't hear the gun go off when you pull the trigger.

Maxwell Alexander Drake, "Wishing You Weren't Here," first appeared in *Wish You Were Here: Stories and Essays Inspired by Fabulous Las Vegas Postcards*, 2012. Reprinted with permission.

12

The Overshadow

McKel Jensen

"HURRY. Come on, little one. Hurry up. Get your coat. We need to leave." The mother's words were not much louder than a whisper as she hurriedly gathered boots and wool mittens for the young girl to put on.

"You, too," she said to a young man. "We must leave now. Come on."

As the mother glanced out the window, she observed that the moon had shifted the shadows away from the cabin. She moved away from the window and pulled the curtain closed. She then promptly placed anything she could into her satchel.

The girl asked, "Did it find us?"

The girl grabbed her ragged doll and placed it clumsily into her pocket with her mittened hand. She had grown to like this place. The cabin, circled by trees, was small, but the stove was warm and the hearth around the metal fireplace was bordered with a mosaic of little purple flowers. And the three of them got to share a small bed in the corner by the table. When they arrived at this location, her older brother immediately claimed the red chair on the north side of the table. It reminded him of the chairs at school back in the city. Hung on the wall behind the chair was a framed work of cross-stitch written in Cyrillic: *The deal was made; price will be paid.* The girl loved the little house stitched under the words she could not read, and she noticed the purple flowers surrounding the cross-stitch house were the same as those on the hearth.

Their mother had just taken dinner out of the oven when she announced they must leave. Then she doused the fire.

"Come on, my son," the mother insisted. "Vlad, watch your sister."

The three pressed over the threshold and out of the door. The cold air stung the hair in their noses, bringing with it the stark reality of their plight.

"Watch your step now," the mother reminded them as she bundled her scarf tighter around her face to shield it from the cold. "Stay where the ground is lit."

Only one lane led away from this cabin. It was long and wide enough for a small car if they'd had one, but no wider. The lane was straight. It led away from the cabin and down the hill. The fresh snow blanketed the layer of snow that had already accumulated. This indicated that there had been nobody in the area for days—no tracks, no compaction.

Night had fallen and with it the forest shadows expanded across the path, almost reaching the other side, thus making the trees look as if they had more to cover, more to hide.

The mother tried to make sense of the darkness between the trees, but that darkness gave no answers. If the mother had a keener sense, she would have seen the shadow move—like the silhouette of tentacles or the elongated arms of a two-dimensional soul—as it kept up with their pace, observing from the trees.

"Mama, how much farther?" the older boy asked.

"We can't be concerned about that right now, my love," Mother said. "We will get there when we do."

The mother hesitated. It was unusual for her son to complain like this. From her satchel she produced a quarter loaf of bread wrapped in a cloth rag.

"Vlad, here," she said. "Eat this, but do so quickly and quietly." She peered around herself and listened before adding, "And please share with your sister. She could use the strength."

In the light of the moon, the children ate what they could, careful not to let even a crumb fall from their hands. Moments passed, and the three continued on their way with no choice but to ignore the bite the air left on their faces and the sluggishness of their frozen feet.

"What kind of moon is that, Mama?" the girl asked. "Did we leave on a full moon?"

"Now quiet, my love." The mother spoke urgently, but she knew this long travel must be treacherous for the mind, let alone the body, of her daughter, so she entertained softly and directly. "It's called a gibbous moon," she continued. "It's not quite a full moon yet."

A snapping sound made them halt on their path, huddled together for warmth as much as for safety. The slight distraction of conversation was over. The mother looked keenly for the source of the sound while guarding her children. She stood there, erect, solid, until she concluded it was safe to continue walking. Something felt familiar, déjà vu-like, yet she had never traveled along this path before, and knew only one lane traveled from that cabin. They had crossed no other trail.

Hours elapsed as the three moved downhill to their destination. They could no longer see the moon, yet its incomplete reflection filtered through the tops of the trees. The reflection from the lunar face gave them enough light to see, but made the darkness around them unforgiving. It was hard to tell where the forest ended and the shadows began.

"Stop, children," the mother said urgently, pointing to the path ahead of them. Their illuminated trail had been obstructed by the shadow stretching across the road's entire width, just five meters ahead. Slowly, the mother crouched down and took up a small stone. With deliberate movements, she threw the stone toward the shadow and watched it land and roll right into the darkness. Without letting her eyes leave the spot where she knew the stone had landed, she watched. It was subtle, but she saw it.

"There," she told the children. "Look. There. Do you see it?"

The children watched as the shadow flickered. It was like the shadows cast by a solar eclipse, but it was nighttime, and no such thing could happen at night. As they watched, they saw a quick, smooth, tentacle sweep out and back, surrounding the spot where the stone had landed.

The children gasped.

"It's gone, isn't it, Mama?" the girl asked.

"Yes, my dear," the mother said, trying to not display the fear that was reaching up in her throat. "We will wait here," she said. The mother looked to the sky to observe the illumination from the moon, trying to determine how much time they could spare before either continuing on their way or freezing to death.

"Oh, sweet love," the mother exclaimed. "Look there."

The shadow had moved just enough for them to get through on one side.

"Little one," she said, "line up closely to your brother. I'll follow behind you, but we need to move quickly."

The three lined up single-file and stepped lightly across the edge of the darkness that had crossed their path. The girl stopped to stare into the darkness before feeling her brother's tug.

As they continued, the shadow grew longer, making that part of their journey all the more hazardous.

Then they became more aware of the road in front of them. Soon they came to a clearing.

"Look there, children," she pointed out into the distance, straight ahead. Smoke billowed out of the chimney of a small cabin encircled by trees but illuminated in the moonlight. The cabin's own shadow stretched beyond the path of the arriving visitors.

"Stomp your feet," the mother said to the girl as they walked over the threshold. "Try not to get any snow in the house."

Relieved for the reprieve of the cold, the mother and two children unwrapped themselves and looked around. The cabin was small but warm. It had a table and one red chair.

"Mama," said the girl, inspecting the room, "look at these flowers around the hearth." She touched the delicate mosaics by the metal fireplace. "Purple is my favorite color," she said. "Isn't it beautiful?"

The mother looked out of the curtained window then turned her attention inside the cabin and noticed the small bed in the corner by the table.

Outside, the trees' shadows grew over the cabin. A small flicker of an overshadow climbed up and blanketed the roof, encircling the home with its outstretched arms clasping its hands at the door.

"It is, my love," the mother answered. "We will be safe here."

13

The Last Man
Gabriel Taylor

EIGHTEEN INCHES. A foot and a half of soil I have to remove before I can plant anything. A foot and a half of soil I can't touch with my skin. A foot and a half of dust and sand I can't breathe if I want to live. That's what the book says, the book I found down here. There really isn't much here besides a couple weeks' worth of food and water along with some batteries, a flashlight, first-aid kit, and the book. I'm supposed to wait here until I have three days of food and water left, and then I run for it. I have to get away, get to the rendezvous point as quick as I can. I hope I can remember which way is north from here. That's important, too. There's so much to remember, so many important things. If I forget one of them, do something wrong, I'm dead. Oh, God, watch over me.

———

How did it come to this? Did they think they would survive? Did anyone else survive? Who knows? Maybe they did survive.

Lucky them. I shouldn't have survived. I only had a few seconds to get to the bunker before everything went to hell. I had no choice but to shut the doors. I waited inside, listening to the roar of the holocaust without. Lucky me.

———

It's warm down here and the air tastes stale. It's too early to go up, but I wonder. I've lasted so far. Three days, I think. There's supposed to be filters down here to keep the air breathable, but I can't find them. Maybe they're hidden to keep them protected. There are vents but I don't feel any air moving. If I get too tired and feel like I'm going to pass out, I'll have to go up. The book says that if anything goes wrong with the filters, I'll have five days of air down here if I stay calm and limit movement. Less if I'm nervous and fidgety. I may have to move tomorrow. Can't stop my hands from shaking.

———

Potassium iodide pills. They look like horse pills. As big as quarters, almost. I hate pills. Oh well. I can't stay down here another day; I'm getting cooked. And the air is going bad. I found an O2 meter behind the first-aid kit. That's why I have to take the potassium pills. The air above may still be full of dust. I'll have my face mask, but I'm bound to get some of it in my lungs. Hopefully, the pills will block it from getting into my lymph nodes or whatever. I don't understand how any of this works. I'm just following what the book says. I'll leave tonight. Everyone dies sooner or later. I wonder if dying down here is really any worse than out there.

————

I made it, so far. It took me over two days but I made it. The radiation counter sang when I stuck my head up, but now it only beeps occasionally. Everything itches, but the book says to not give in. I can't spare any water for a bath, either, so I have to live with it. I have a couple more days' worth of food and water. I'll need to find more.

————

The book said there were some other bunkers nearby. I hoped to find people here. But there's no one, and the bunkers weren't sealed before the blast so the supplies are ruined. The sky is dark nearly all the time, and thunderstorms constantly loom on the horizon. The lightning in them scares me. I've never seen anything so powerful. Lights up the entire horizon. Nothing looks familiar now. There are mountains and valleys every-where, and they use to be plains. If the storms come too much closer, I'll have to move again. Rain doesn't help anything grow now. It only kills.

————

I moved on two days ago and found a bunker today. The doors were shut but not locked. No one inside. I have more supplies now.

————

Been here a few days. The storms are still on the horizon. I stay down in the bunker most of the time, waiting. The book says the nearest rendezvous point is a little further north from here. As far as I can remember, there aren't any more cities between here and there. Just small towns. No shelters, fewer supplies, and to go north means getting closer to the storms.

———

Deep down, I think we all knew it would come to this. We just didn't know when it would come. There wasn't any warning. On my way to work, alarms started going off, and I happened to be next to the bunker. In the beginning, I wondered if it would come by accident. Now I see things clearly, how frightened people were, how desperate. Some wanted this to happen, believed it was the only way. In war, lots of people pull the trigger but only a few have blood on their hands.

———

I think I'm dying. Part of me wants to. Blisters cover most of my body. Even with all the pain, I managed to run when the storms came. I've never seen a sky change so fast. The dark clouds thrashed around as the thunder shrieked. There were still a few buildings standing nearby. They're not there anymore, but I survived. The rain was cold even though it felt like it was boiling. I ran north through it all. The storms came from the north, so I might have shaved off a few minutes or maybe even an hour from the time I had to spend in the storm, but I might have shaved more than that off my own life. I took more potassium. It may help.

———

I found them today. The others. They're all dead. The air filters in their bunker must not have worked, either. There were so many of them down there. Their air must have run out after a couple hours. I don't have the strength to bury them. I guess a bunker's as good as anything now. There's another rendezvous point to the east, then one more north of that. I have to keep moving. The rain makes my radiation counter sing. I think I'm bleeding inside.

———

For the last couple of days I haven't been able to eat. I've been throwing up constantly, and there's blood mixed in the bile. I managed some water today, but I have to ration it. I can't waste what I have. It isn't much. The sores on my arms and legs have begun to heal, at least. I keep taking the potassium pills. I feel better when I do, but that may just be a placebo. My radiation counter still chirps regularly. There's only a couple miles before the next rendezvous point. I travel as far as I can each day. It may take me a while.

———

Well, I'm still alive. That's something, at least. The batteries in my radiation counter are dying. I can only turn it on once in a while to check if I'm safe. The storms seem to be calming down. I feel a lot better, too. I'm not so shaky as I was before, either. I've made it to the second rendezvous point. Same problem as the others. At least I'm not running out of supplies for now.

———

I don't know why I'm writing this. I've been wondering about it the last couple of days. I don't know what got me started, but now I don't know if I can stop. Not until I either find the others or I die. I don't care which it is. I don't want to live like this. It may be childish, but I can't bare this solitude. I don't speak aloud anymore because I'm afraid I won't stop talking to myself. My family lived near the last rendezvous point. Maybe they're still alive. Perhaps it's foolish of me to get my hopes up. I do hope.

————

I was married, once. That doesn't matter now, I know, but I thought I should write it down. We never had any children. I regret that now.

————

I'm half a mile from the rendezvous point, I think. Smoke rises from that direction. Tomorrow I should reach them, if my strength holds out. Ever since the rain I've been so tired and weak. I didn't want to admit it. A couple hours of walking is all I've been able to manage the last few days. I'm too exhausted to do much more. Hopefully, that rising smoke is from camp fires. The book says this shelter could house hundreds of refugees and even has a medical facility. Maybe I'll finally find the others, find my family. Maybe I'll be dead before I get there.

————

Thought I'd take a rest before I climb this last hill. I should be able to see the rendezvous point from the top. If they're not there, then I'll know that this must be my penance, my hell, to wander through this dead world. I hope they're alive. So tired. I'll take a nap and then climb the last hill.

Gabriel Taylor, "The Last Man," first appeared in *Words to Paint With*, 2012. Reprinted with permission.

About the Authors

Eric Bishop is a dad to four, husband to one, and grandpa to three. His debut novel, *The Samaritan's Pistol*, was called "Taut, refreshing and well-paced" by Publisher's Weekly. Long on imagination but short on writing skills, he credits the Cache Valley chapter of the League of Utah Writers for helping him learn everything needed to get published.

Maxwell Alexander Drake, or Drake as he prefers to be called, is an award-winning Science Fiction/Fantasy author and Graphic Novelist. He is best known for his fantasy series, The Genesis of Oblivion Saga. He teaches Creative Writing all around the country at schools, libraries, writers' conferences and fan events. You can learn more about his writing lessons, as well as keep up to date on his upcoming projects, at his official website, www.maxwellalexanderdrake.com.

McKel Jensen was inspired by her time walking a tree-lined path at night on the outskirts of St. Petersburg, Russia. She wrote what scared her: the unknown watching from the shadows. McKel currently lives in Brigham City with her husband and believes maybe she should write more of what scares her: parenting. She is the mother of three perfectly inspiring, too smart for their own good, young kids. McKel is a member of the Brigham City Writers' chapter of the League of Utah Writers.

Tim Keller is an avid reader who also has a weak spot for monster movies. He likes traveling, 80's music, and if the highway patrol is to be believed, driving way too fast. After working as a bouncer, mortgage researcher, computer repair technician, caregiver, and a brief, albeit disastrous, stint as a waiter in anachronistic drag, he decided he wanted to be a writer when he grew up. A keen observer of human nature, Tim enjoys writing stories about all kinds of people from all walks of life. His work can be found in various literary journals and anthologies including *Mirrored Realities, In the Shimmering, Between Places*, and the *Helicon West Anthology*.

Although he has been writing most of his life, **Mike Nelson** didn't get serious until he retired in 2014. His third novel, *Clairvoyant*, was awarded the League of Utah Writer's Silver Quill for adult literature in 2019. *Clairvoyant: Book 2* is his fifth published novel. He has also published numerous short stories. Mike served in the U.S. Air Force and is the proud father of six children, an active member of his church, and currently lives with his wife of fifty-one years in Northern Utah.

Alexander Gordon Smith is the award-winning author of a number of bestselling children's and young adult books, including *The Inventors*, the Escape From Furnace series, and *The Fury*. He is the author of two creative writing handbooks, *Inspired Creative Writing* and *Writing Bestselling Children's Books*, a number of screenplays, several non-fiction books and hundreds of short stories and articles. Gordon is the founder of Egg Box Publishing, an independent, non-profit imprint designed to publish and promote talented new writers and poets, and is the co-owner of Fear Driven Films.

TJ Tarbet is an avid reader, writer, martial artist, and role player. In fact, the first actual piece of fiction he wrote was for a home-brew Dungeons and Dragons campaign that he ran with his friends and family. It wasn't excellent, and he soon lost control of the group, but it helped him realize that crafting stories was a lot easier when you didn't have to worry about those pesky players. Some of his favorite authors include Cormac McCarthy, Madeline Le'Engle, Brandon Sanderson, Robert Jordan, and Glen Cook.

Gabriel Taylor loves telling stories that are surprising, often fanciful, and deal with the themes of life, death, and the desires that drive us all. Gabriel is currently focused on writing short stories and finishing a novel on his website, but he has also written screenplays for a number of independent films and collections of poetry in the past.

You can read more of his work at www.patreon.com/gabrieltaylor_storyteller

Isaac Timm was born and raised in the western desert town of Callao, Utah; a stop on the historic Pony Express trail. His highest aspiration is to be a story teller like his father. He is a graduate of Utah State University in history and English. His poetry and short stories have won numerous awards.

Chadd VanZanten writes narrative nonfiction essays and literary short stories, no one of which is really much truer than any of the others. His fiction has been published in numerous anthologies, including *Creep Factor: Thirteen Deeply Creepy Horror Stories* (Knowledge Forest Press 2018), and in his short-story collection *The Key To This Whole Entire Thing* (Knowledge

Forest Press 2019). He is also the author of works on fly-fishing and backpacking, including *On Fly-Fishing The Wind Rivers* (The History Press 2018).

E.B. Wheeler is the award-winning author of twelve books, including *Wishwood, Moon Hollow,* and *The Haunting of Springett Hall,* as well as several short stories, magazine articles, and scripts for educational software programs. You can find more about her books at https://www.amazon.com/E.B.-Wheeler/e/B00VKQG6MO or ebwheeler.com

Printed in Great Britain
by Amazon

14435911R00118